"I pro[mise you]'ll [not be] kidnap[...]"

Jaime jerked away from him.

The physical ad[...] stood against the clo[...] room door. "I don't suppose you'd believe m[e if] I said I'd like to keep you safe."

She studied the man she'd first considered a hunk. In any other situation, she would have found him attractive in a rugged, risky sort of way. His jaw line was craggy, his physique muscular. His short, thick hair was blue-black, like midnight on a moonless night.

But it was his eyes, piercing yet shadowed with mysterious incongruities, that got to her the most. They tempted her to believe there really might be more than evil lurking behind those burning depths.

But could she afford to find out?

"I promise you'll rue the day you kidnapped me."

James jerked free of Rio's grasp and stumbled away from him, bracing herself to fight him off.

The physical advances didn't come. Instead he strode across the closed bedroom and said, "I'm going to lock you in here if I send Zio like it or not."

COWBOY DELIRIUM

BY
JOANNA WAYNE

First published in Great Britain 2011
Harlequin Mills & Boon Limited,
Eton House, 18-24 Paradise Road, Richmond, Surrey TW9 1SR

COWBOY DELIRIUM © Jo Ann Vest 2010

ISBN: 978 0 263 88509 5

46-0211

Harlequin Mills & Boon policy is to use papers that are natural, renewable
and recyclable products and made from wood grown in sustainable forests.
The logging and manufacturing processes conform to the legal environmental
regulations of the country of origin.

Printed and bound in Spain
by Litografia Rosés S.A., Barcelona

Joanna Wayne was born and raised in Shreveport, Louisiana, and received her undergraduate and graduate degrees from LSU-Shreveport. She moved to New Orleans in 1984, and it was there that she attended her first writing class and joined her first professional writing organization. Her debut novel was published in 1994.

Now, dozens of published books later, Joanna has made a name for herself as being on the cutting edge of romantic suspense in both series and single-title novels. She has been on the Waldenbooks bestseller list for romance and has won many industry awards. She is also a popular speaker at writing organisations and local community functions and has taught creative writing at the University of New Orleans Metropolitan College.

Joanna currently resides in a small community forty miles north of Houston, Texas, with her husband. Though she still has many family and emotional ties to Louisiana, she loves living in the Lone Star State. You may write to Joanna at PO Box 265, Montgomery, Texas 77356.

This book is dedicated to all my loyal readers who couldn't get enough of the Collingsworth family and asked repeatedly when Jaime would get her man. Also to America's brave law enforcement officers and military personnel who sacrifice so much to keep us safe. And to my hubby for cooking dinner for me when I get so busy writing I forget to do it for him.

Chapter One

"Surely you can't be cruel enough to send me away without so much as a nightcap?"

Jaime Collingsworth found that difficult to believe herself. A full moon, a gorgeous, fascinating man who was hot for her, and she was going to dismiss him with a kiss at her door. But duty called—and had left two messages.

"We've been out late every night this week," she reminded him.

"I know," he said, slipping his arm along the back of the car seat to massage her shoulder. "But I have this serious problem. I simply can't get enough of you."

"Slow down, tiger. No need to rush the romance. And I absolutely have to get up in time tomorrow to make it to Jack's Bluff for Sunday brunch. I haven't been to the ranch in four weeks, and my mother is on my case big time."

Actually Jaime missed her mother as well. Her family was huge and could be overwhelming, but still, she was looking forward to visiting with all of them, especially her young nieces and nephews. Her new Houston townhouse was great, but Jack's Bluff Ranch was home.

"You could take me with you," Buerto said. "I'd love to meet your family, especially that cantankerous grandpa you keep talking about."

"So you keep saying, but I hate those meet-the-family occasions. They are far too stressful."

"You sound as if you've had a lot of them."

"Not so many." But enough that she hated to go through the ordeal when she didn't have to. "It could be fun, though," she teased. "You'd be sized up more thoroughly than a new bull being introduced to the herd."

"Four protective cowboy brothers checking me out and one of them an armed law enforcement officer," Buerto said. "Why does that not amuse me the way it does you?"

"They *all* have guns," Jaime said. "But it's my mother you'd really have to worry about."

Buerto waited for the gate to her townhouse complex to open and then drove inside. He slowed as they passed the sparkling fountain, English gardens and finally the privacy border of thick shrubbery.

He stopped in front of her three-story townhouse. "I'll assure your mother that my intentions are honorable."

"It won't help. She knows mine never are."

That wasn't exactly true, but it was close enough. Jaime liked guys. She just never fell in love, at least not the way her sister, Becky, and her brothers had.

For her, men were more like a new pair of Manolo

Blahnik shoes or a Roberto Cavalli gown. They were intoxicatingly seductive when first acquired, but lost their glamour and excitement when the newness wore off.

There was an outside chance it could be different with Buerto—which was reason enough not to throw him to the wolves this early in the relationship.

She shifted in her seat, letting the short skirt of her sky-blue dress inch up to mid-thigh for Buerto's benefit as she reached for the door handle.

He leaned across the seat and kissed her before sliding out his side of the car to walk her to the door.

Once up the short walk, he slipped his arms around her and pulled her close. His advance was interrupted by a black sedan that skidded to a stop behind his silver Porsche.

The doors flew open and three men jumped out. One of the men was short and slightly balding. Another was tall with a crooked scar that ran from his right temple to the center of his cheek. The third was a certified hunk, hard bodied, clean shaven, cocky swagger. And holding a gun.

Panic ripped through her. She and Buerto were about to be robbed. She scanned the area. No one was in sight, and she knew her closest neighbor was out of town.

Two of the men went for Buerto, shoving him backward and pinning his arms against the front wall of her house.

Jaime tore her handbag from her shoulder and threw it into the driveway. "Take the money. Please. Just take it and go."

The hunky guy wrapped an arm around her and started dragging her to the car. "We're taking you with us. Better if you don't put up a fight."

"Take your hands off her," Buerto yelled.

The effort to save her earned him a punch in the face. The shorter assailant shoved him to the pavement and kicked him in the stomach before grabbing Jaime's purse and keys.

Then he put a gun to Buerto's head. "If you go to the cops, your girlfriend's as good as dead. Tell that to her family. We'll be in touch."

The man who held her lifted her and threw her into the backseat of the car. She got in one swift knee to the crotch that narrowly missed its target.

The taller guy was waiting for her in the car. He reached over and she felt a sharp prick in her forearm. A needle.

"Handle her, Rio," the needle wielder barked as he climbed out of the backseat.

The hunky thug slid in beside her.

Not about to give in without a fight, she sank her teeth into his shoulder and bit down as hard as she could. He barely winced, but he quickly closed his hand over her mouth and gripped it so firmly she couldn't even part her lips.

Her vision had begun to blur—no doubt from whatever was in that syringe—but she caught a glimpse of Buerto as they sped away. He was groveling on the ground in obvious pain. He hadn't died trying to defend her. At least there was that.

The man beside her looked her in the eye, and the intensity of his gaze seemed to crawl inside her. He put his mouth to her ear. "Trust me, and you'll get out of this alive."

She'd sooner trust a viper. Her eyes grew heavy and her head begin to spin. This could not be happening to her.

Except that it was.

Chapter Two

Zach Collingsworth pushed through the front door of the big house carrying four cold beers. He handed one to each of his three brothers and then took a big gulp of the last one before propping his backside against the porch railing. God, it felt good to be home after three weeks combing dusty Texas border towns.

"So what's up with your new task force assignment?" his brother Langston asked. "Are you getting a handle on curbing the violence?"

"It's hard to say," Zach admitted. "A week ago two border patrol agents were killed, assassination style, in the driveways of their own homes. The week before that, an innocent kid was killed in a drive-by. This week, nothing."

"Any arrests?" his brother Matt asked.

"No. That's the worst part. There were witnesses to the kid getting killed but no one's willing to talk for fear of retribution. And there's no evidence as to who took out the border patrol officers other than it looks like the work of the drug cartels."

"So we're still losing the war on domestic terrorism right here in our own state," Bart said. "This is not the world I want my infant son to grow up in."

"We'll stop it," Zach said. "Texans always come out on top. You know that. I'm just worried about how many innocent people will die before we do."

Langston took a swig of beer and then caught hold of one of the chains that held the porch swing, giving it a rattling shake. "Make sure you're not one of those victims, Zach. You've got a lot to live for."

"So did the agents who went down. But believe me I'm not planning on making my beautiful wife a widow anytime soon. So how's the oil business?" he asked Langston, ready to change the subject. He'd shared about all he could anyway. The operations of the newly formed task force were mostly confidential.

"We're feeling the financial pinch like everyone else, but we're still economically sound."

"And the cattle business?" Zach asked, turning his attention to Matt and Bart, who co-managed Jack's Bluff Ranch.

Before they could answer, the hum of a motor sounded in the distance. All their gazes immediately redirected to the curving dirt ranch road leading to the house.

Zach pushed up the sleeve of the pale shirt Kali had bought for him in the new western shop in Colts Run Cross last week. "Nearly midnight. Awful late for company."

"Sign of trouble," Bart said. "Probably one of the

neighbors needing help bringing a troublesome calf into the world."

Tension settled in the pit of Zach's stomach. Over the last few weeks the word *trouble* had taken on much darker connotations for him. He checked his cell phone. No new messages from Kali since she'd called to tell him that she'd made it back to their neighboring ranch and that her pregnant mare showed no sign of foaling before morning.

Kali had left him at Jack's Bluff to bond with his brothers over beer and conversation. She knew he needed that. Kali had a way of always knowing what he needed. More often than not what he needed was her.

He didn't recognize the low-slung silver sports car that came into view and then slowed as it approached the house. "Not a neighbor," he said, "unless one of them just bought a new Porsche."

"Ten bucks says the driver's lost," Matt said.

Bart stretched and stood from his perch on the porch railing. "Lost or looking for Jaime. There's a full moon tonight and that seems to bring out all her jilted Texas exes."

"Poor suckers," Zach said. His twin sister did have a habit of leaving a string of broken hearts in her wake.

A lean, slightly muscled man jumped from the car when it stopped and strode toward them. When he stepped into the circle of light from the porch, it was clear he'd been in a fight and probably not come out the winner.

Langston walked down the steps to meet him. "Can we help you?"

"I'm here about Jaime."

Zach's stomach clenched as he stepped to Langston's side. There was no way this could be good. "What about her?"

"She's been kidnapped."

An ominous, choking silence hovered just long enough for them to get their minds around the pronouncement. Then the questions started flying all at once.

"When?"

"Was she hurt?"

"Kidnapped by whom?"

"How do you know this?"

"Who the hell are you?"

The stranger put his hand up as if the questions were blows. "Are you her brothers?"

"Yeah," Matt said. "Now start talking."

"Okay, but I'm on your side. My name's Buerto Arredondo. Jaime works for me."

"You're the art collector?"

He nodded. "I'm in the States to buy art for a resort I'm building just outside Mexico City." He pulled a handkerchief from his back pocket and wiped a stream of sweat from his brow.

"Tell us what happened to Jaime," Zack insisted impatiently. He didn't give a damn what this guy did or didn't collect.

"We'd visited an art gallery in the Heights this

evening and then gone to dinner. I was walking her to her door when three men jumped us. I tried to stop them but I couldn't fight off all of them. They threw Jaime in the back of their car and took off."

"Did she know them?"

"No, but I'm pretty sure they knew who she is. They said if I went to the police they would kill her. I was told to make certain her family got that same warning."

Zach muttered a curse and slammed his right fist into his left hand. "Not again." It hadn't even been two years since they'd had to rescue his nephews, Derrick and David, from a lunatic. It was like they'd become a target for all the crazies in the world.

"Did the kidnappers say anything else?" he asked. "Did they give any clue as to who they were or when they would contact us?"

"Nothing."

"Did they hurt Jaime?"

"They manhandled her. That's all I saw but who knows what they're capable of. You have no choice but to cooperate with them."

"That's not your decision to make," Langston said. His voice was firm. He was the oldest brother, the leader of the family, a responsibility he took seriously.

Zach didn't question his intelligence or abilities, but kidnapping was a criminal act and that put this squarely in Zach's saddle. Besides, Jaime was his twin. As different as they were in many aspects, he shared a bond with her that none of the others did.

"Start at the first, Mr. Arredondo," Zach said, "and tell us every detail. Leave nothing out, no matter how unimportant it may seem."

"Please, call me Buerto. And I think you should know that I am not only your sister's boss."

"What's that supposed to mean?"

"We're in a relationship, a very close relationship. I care a great deal for her. This is as hard on me as it is on you."

Zach didn't fully buy that, but all that mattered now was getting Jaime home safely. Whoever the sons of bitches were that abducted her, they'd just taken on the whole Collingsworth clan, and even Buerto Arredondo had best not get in their way.

LENORA WOKE TO THE SOUND of male voices coming from the kitchen below her bedroom and the odor of freshly perked coffee. She rolled over and checked the time on her bedside clock. Twelve twenty-eight.

It wasn't all that unusual for her sons to talk past midnight. With Zack working on that new task force, it had been weeks since they'd all been together. But she didn't recall their ever making coffee this late—unless something was wrong.

That fact forced the last dregs of sleep from her eyes. Kicking back the sheet, she threw her legs over the side of the bed and padded to her closet for her robe.

She picked up on the unfamiliar voice as she approached the kitchen. A cold shudder stampeded through her nerves when she heard him mention Jaime's name. Had there been a wreck? Had she been riding that motorbike Lenora hated so much?

Pushing through the door, Lenora planted herself in the center of the kitchen and stared at the stranger sipping coffee from one of her blue pottery mugs. Her gaze left him to scrutinize each of her sons, reading the turbulence that clouded their eyes.

"What's wrong? What's happened to Jaime?"

Langston wrapped an arm around her shoulder. "Sit down, Mom."

She yanked from his grasp. "I don't need to sit down. Was there a wreck? Is Jaime in the hospital? Is she hurt?"

"She's been abducted."

Lenora's chest contracted until she could barely breathe. There had to be some kind of mistake. Everyone loved Jaime. No one would hurt her. She stared at the stranger again. "Who are you?"

"This is Jaime's boss," Zach said. "He was with her when three men attacked them and left with Jaime. He's only here to help."

Lenora grabbed the man's arms. "You let them take my daughter? You let them take Jaime?"

"I tried to stop them," he said.

Matt pulled his mother into his arms. "He's here to help, Mom. We'll get Jaime back. You can count on that. Just try to stay calm while we think this through."

The empty words of reassurance roared in her head and a pain so intense it blinded her jabbed through her heart. Her chest exploded, and her mind went off in a million fiery tangents.

The pain hit again, and this time she felt herself crashing against the table. Jaime's face appeared for a second and then vanished in a frigid swirl of black.

TWO HOURS AFTER THE ABDUCTION, the black sedan turned onto an isolated, muddy logging road that didn't appear to have been used in years. In the backseat Rio Hernandez was still fuming at the turn of events and the lack of warning he'd had about what was going down. Not only did this not advance his own agenda, it put a serious kink in it.

"Where the hell are we going?" Rio demanded. "Or is that top secret, too?"

"There's an old fishing camp at the end of the road," Poncho answered from the driver seat. "You two beasts and the beauty will hold up there until we hear otherwise."

The front right tire plunged into a deep pothole and the car shuddered and jerked, throwing the semiconscious prisoner against Rio's shoulder.

He steadied her, aware of the softness of her skin beneath his hand and the silky texture of her hair as it brushed his rough cheek. His insides revolted at the quick stir of attraction. Definitely not the time for his libido to get into the act.

The woman's eyes fluttered open and she looked up, meeting Rio's gaze. Confusion clouded the deep blue of her irises, making her appear far more vulnerable than she'd looked when sinking her sharp white teeth into the sinewy tissue of his shoulder.

A gurgle resonated from deep in her throat, capturing the attention of the other passenger in the car. From the front Luke turned so that he could see into the backseat. "You two getting all cozy back there?" A croaking laugh punctuated what he saw as an amusing comment.

"What's it to you?" Rio quipped.

"No one gave you first dibs on her," Luke retorted.

"She ain't up for dibs," Poncho said. "She's not entertainment. She's collateral. Get it?"

"Yeah, we get it," Rio said. "So is this hottie worth going to prison for?"

"No one's going to prison on her account, not unless you guys foul things up. Then you still won't have to worry. You won't live long enough to face a judge and jury."

Two miles farther and the road played out completely. Poncho finally pulled to a stop in a cluster of towering pine trees. Just beyond them, a ramshackle cabin with a leaning chimney and a half-rotted stoop waited unwelcomingly.

"This is home for the next few days," Poncho said.

Rio opened the car door and stepped into a soggy bed of pine straw. "This dump? No self-respecting rat would stay here."

Luke screwed his lips into a scowl as he climbed from the front seat. "I'm not sleeping with rats."

"You've slept with worse," the driver commented.

Luke worried the scar on his face and stepped over

a downed limb. "You aren't going to leave us stranded out here in the middle of nowhere, are you?"

Poncho reached into his pocket and pulled out a key ring with one key attached. He tossed it to Luke.

"There's a car parked out of sight behind the cabin, but you're to stay put until you get word to drive the woman somewhere. When you do, tie her, gag her and lock her in the trunk. There's rope and duct tape ready and waiting."

"Looks like the end of the friggin' world," Luke said. "Phones aren't going to work out here."

"Your phones will work. It's all been checked out. They're essential to the plan's execution." Poncho scratched his balding head and swatted at a mosquito feeding on his cheek. "Help the lady inside," he ordered, directing his command at Rio.

Rio tugged the woman from the car and half carried, half dragged her toward the cabin. She was in no shape to offer resistance, but she didn't help, either.

It was more like dragging a dead weight along beside him and he had to be careful not to let her feet get caught in the scratchy brambles that had overgrown the path. Once inside, he let her slide from his grasp into a faded arm chair.

Luke went to the kitchen corner of the main living area and started rummaging through nearly empty cabinets, slamming the doors in disgust as he went. "What are we supposed to eat?"

"Those boxes in the trunk have food and water in them."

"That's more like it." Luke went back for the goods, giving Rio the opportunity he'd been waiting for.

"Is this about a ransom or a payback?" he asked Poncho.

"A ransom. If it were payback, she'd be dead."

"Who's the victim?"

"Jaime Collingsworth."

"Collingsworth as in Collingsworth Oil?"

"Could be."

"So this is about money?"

"You'll find that out if and when you need to know."

"I didn't sign on to be treated like a second-class citizen."

"You do as you're told, Rio."

"That's not how it was explained to me. I'm a Navy SEAL. We don't play the role of flunky."

"You *were* a SEAL. Now you're just the new guy on the block. The boss wants proof you're a hundred percent before he invites you to the dinner table."

"Carlos would have never thrown me a crumb if he hadn't checked me out fully. I was told I'd be a key player."

Poncho leaned on the short counter that separated the kitchen from the rest of the room. "This kidnapping is big, Rio. See this through without a glitch, and you'll see plenty of action next time from the inside out. And your bonus will make all the trouble worthwhile."

"I'll see it through, but I don't want any more surprises like the abduction tonight. And I'd just as soon you take that buffoon with you when you leave." He nodded toward the door where Luke had stepped outside. "He'll be nothing but trouble for me."

"Luke's not as dumb as he seems. And the boss trusts him to do as he's told without talking. That counts."

Carlos might trust Luke, but Rio didn't, especially now that he had the sexy spitfire thrown into the mix. Any way he looked at it she was solid trouble. When the pin is pulled, Mr. Grenade is not your friend.

Odd how that old Murphy's Law of military combat came back to haunt him even now.

He needed more information about the woman, and he wasn't going to get it from Poncho. That meant he needed a minute without Luke hanging over his shoulder. He had to bide his time.

When Luke returned to guard the victim, Poncho and Rio did a quick walk-through of the small cabin.

There were two bedrooms, one with a couple of twin beds, the other with a double bed. The one window in that room had been securely boarded up. The door locked with a key from the outside. No doubt this was Jaime's room.

The furnishings in Jaime's temporary prison consisted of the bed with a saggy mattress and pine bedside table topped with a cypress-knee lamp that looked as if it had been crafted by a six-year-old. Rio flicked on the lamp. To his surprise it worked.

A pine rocker with a deerskin seat sat next to the door that led to a bathroom the size of a small broom closet. It held only a toilet and a stained sink. The rusting medicine cabinet on the wall was missing a cover. It had been mirrored, Rio surmised, and removed so that Jaime couldn't break it and use a jagged sliver of the glass as a weapon.

Jaime had revived enough that she was sitting up straight in the chair when Poncho finally took his leave. She pulled her arms over her chest and looked Rio in the eye. "Whatever he's paying you to keep me here, I can pay you more to let me go."

Luke walked over and propped on the arm of her chair and stroked her chin with a slightly crooked finger. "Now why would we want to let a pretty lady like you leave?"

She shoved his hand away. "Because if you don't, my brothers will find you and kill you."

"Yeah, well, your brothers aren't here now, are they, sweet thing? It's just you and us."

Rio stiffened. "Let up, Luke."

"Don't get so huffed up. No one said she's yours."

"I'm saying it." Rio walked over and tugged Jaime to a standing position. He pulled her close and let his hand cup her firm buttock so that Luke didn't miss the message. "You're off duty now, Luke. I'm taking over for the night." He led Jaime toward the bedroom.

She snarled as he pushed her inside, her words still a bit slurred when she said, "Go ahead. Get your filthy kicks, but I promise you'll rue the day forever that you kidnapped me."

Rio figured that was a damn safe bet.

Chapter Three

Jaime jerked free of Rio's grasp and stumbled away from him, bracing herself to fight him off. Not that she could. She'd have never broken free at all if he hadn't intentionally loosened his grip on her arm.

The physical advances didn't come. Instead the man stood with his back against the closed bedroom door. "Don't worry," he said. "All I want from you, Jaime Collingsworth, is a few answers."

Relief left her weak, but tension still crackled in the stuffy, dimly lit room. He knew her name. That didn't surprise her. "I thought you had all the answers."

"I'm working on it. Tell me about your family."

"What about them?"

"Are they wealthy?"

"No," she quipped. "They're dirt poor and mean. Rattlesnake mean."

"So that's where you get your winning personality. Let's start over and this time, stick to the truth."

"Why, because you'll do something drastic like kidnap me and lock me up in a filthy, disgusting room if I lie?"

"I don't suppose you'd believe me if I said I'd like to keep you safe."

She studied the man she'd first considered a hunk. In any other situation, she would have found him attractive in a rugged, risky sort of way. His jawline was craggy, his physique muscular without having the exaggerated features of a body builder.

He was taller than Buerto by a good four inches, which put him well over six feet. His short, thick hair was blue-black, like midnight on a moonless night.

But it was his eyes, the color of rich cognac, piercing yet shadowed with mysterious incongruities, that got to her the most. They tempted her to believe there really might be more than evil lurking behind those burning depths.

She couldn't afford that luxury.

"The other men called you Rio. Is that your real name or just an alias?"

"It's my name. Tell me about your brothers," he coaxed. "Are they in politics?"

"Yes, and they're very influential. They probably have every Texas Ranger, cop and trooper in the state looking for you right now."

"I wouldn't count on that. And lying to me isn't helping your cause."

"What makes you think I'm lying?"

"Not think. Know. Chalk it up to my experience with conniving enemies."

Jaime sucked in a deep breath, determined not to play into this man's hands. "If you know so little about me, why did you kidnap me? Did you follow Buerto and me from the restaurant?"

"Is Buerto your husband?"

"Yes."

"And I guess you always kiss your husband good night at the door after you've gone out for the evening?"

She sucked in a ragged breath. This was getting her nowhere.

Rio walked across the room and approached the bed. Her heart plummeted and dread sucked the breath from her lungs. She backed away until her body was against the wall.

Rio jerked back the faded quilt, tossing it to the foot of the metal bed. "Mattress is garbage but the sheets look clean enough," he noted.

They looked dingy and disgusting to her. But they'd do, as long as she was the only one crawling between them.

He stepped past her and peered into the bathroom. "I'll see if I can find you a bar of soap and a towel and washcloth. If you need anything else or change your mind about cooperating with me, knock on the door. I'll hear you. That offer is just between the two of us. Tell Luke anything I tell you in confidence and I swear I'll stand back and let him have his way with you."

So the actions in front of Luke had been for her protection. Either he found her undesirable himself or else he wasn't entirely evil. If it was the latter, maybe she could make that work for her.

If it was the former…

Well, who cared that a brute found her resistible?

He turned and walked from the room without looking back, but she heard the key turn in the lock before his footfalls faded in the distance.

Anxiety-fed adrenaline still quickened her pulse and churned in her stomach as a legion of more pressing questions took over her mind.

Was Buerto okay and had he told her family? How had her brothers reacted to the news? Were they planning to cooperate with the kidnappers or had they gone straight to the police or maybe the FBI? Was there a mass manhunt already underway?

How was her mother taking the news?

Jaime's heart constricted at the thought of her mother having to face this kind of worry and fear. She had to find a way to get word to her that she was okay. No, she had to find a way to escape.

She'd never overpower her kidnappers. They were simply too muscular and strong. She'd have to outsmart them. That would be difficult with Rio. He was cagey himself and had already shown that he didn't fall for her lies. If she were to outfox anyone, it would have to be Luke.

She kicked free of her favorite stiletto sandals, for once wishing she'd worn a pair of boring, sensible shoes. Instead she was stuck in the wilderness dressed for a night on the town. That pretty much eliminated making a run for it through the woods.

Something skittered across her bare toes. She looked down as a giant cockroach paraded along her instep. A scream escaped before she could swallow it back.

Before she regained her equilibrium, her door flew open. Rio stormed in as the frightened roach scurried over the bare wooden slats.

He dropped the soap and towels on the bed and stamped on the insect with his booted foot, leaving it a mass of squishy pulp on her floor. This time his lips drew into a half smile.

"Nice to know you're afraid of something, Jaime Collingsworth."

RIO PACED THE BARE FLOORS, almost subconsciously familiarizing himself with the accompanying groans and squeaks. He'd been totally unprepared for the abduction and that concerned him. His BUDs training had prepared him to deal with anything thrown at him, but his years of experience as a frogman had fine-tuned his senses and ability to read even ambiguous clues with precision.

Yet he hadn't suspected the kidnapping.

Still he was convinced that tonight's act was only a prelude to something a lot bigger.

But what?

He needed information on Jaime and the rest of the Collingsworths if he were to figure that out. Jaime clearly wasn't going to just buy his good-guy act and spill any helpful details. He'd have to find enough privacy to make a phone call.

Rio stepped into the dark, narrow hallway, pausing at Jaime's door. The sounds of her rhythmic breathing indicated she'd finally fallen asleep. The unwanted image of her tanned, shapely body stretched out on top of the worn sheets burrowed into his mind. His body reacted as if he'd swallowed a handful of jalapeños.

He shook his head, but the erotic visions didn't budge. Instead they became more distinct. He imagined his fingers tangling in her silky hair, disheveling the blond strands as his lips explored the smooth column of her neck.

Tiptoeing away from her door, he checked on Luke. He was still snoring away, his bare feet sticking out of the tangled sheets of one of the twin beds.

The guy was impulsive, with a quick temper that exploded with little warning. Worse, he was never far from the trigger of his Glock. Nothing like an untimed explosion to foul up a mission.

Rio retraced his path to the kitchen and then stepped onto the back porch, careful to step over gaps left by rotted boards. The lake was only a few yards behind the house, but the towering pines hid it from view. That was no doubt part of the reason the cabin had been chosen as a hideaway. It was virtually invisible from the front or the back until you were right on it.

He walked a few yards of the overgrown path toward the water, then stepped behind the trunk of an aged oak tree. Out of sight and too far away to be overheard if Luke did wake and venture out to look for him, yet close enough he could hear Jaime if she screamed—over a roach or worse.

Bending, he removed the small phone from inside his left boot, his fingers brushing the handle of the hunting knife that rested there in its twin leather sheath. Neither Poncho nor Luke suspected he had this completely private and untraceable mobile device on him.

He placed the call, knowing there would be an almost instant response even at this time of the night. He wasn't disappointed.

"What's up?"

"Trouble."

"Specifics?"

"I've just helped kidnap a woman named Jaime Collingsworth. I'm guessing she's connected to Collingsworth Oil."

"You kidnapped Jaime Collingsworth?" A few curses punctuated the incredulity in his tone.

"I take it that means you know who she is."

"I was good friends with her brother Langston back when we were riding the high school rodeo circuit. Jaime was just a kid then, but I met her on several occasions. And not only do the Collingsworths own Collingsworth Oil, they also have the second biggest ranch in Texas."

So the cartel had taken a major risk in kidnapping Jaime—meaning they expected a bonanza from this. And Rio had ended up right in the middle of it, exactly where he'd hoped to be. Only he hadn't been counting on Jaime to complicate matters.

Rio gathered all the facts he could from the phone call. By the time he'd broken the connection and walked back to the cabin, his head was reeling with the new information, but none of the confusion had been cleared.

He still needed answers and the rest would have to come from the sexy blond spitfire who seemed less afraid of him than she was a cockroach. Every path in sight was mined.

But he'd signed on to do a job. And with a frogman, even a former one, failure was never an option.

IT RAINED SOMETIME during the night, a steady downpour that cleared the pollen from the air and then gave way to the brilliant glow of the morning sun. Even filtered through the layers of grime that smudged the cabin's windows, the rays painted the dingy kitchen in golden streams of light.

Rio checked out the refrigerator for food while Luke sat at the marred kitchen table scratching the toes of his right foot. Jaime was still in her room, though Rio had unlocked it a good half hour ago and told her she was welcome to come out for coffee.

The options for food were limited, but better than Rio had expected. "How about toast, bacon and eggs?" he asked.

"I could go for that," Luke agreed, finally reaching

for his sock, "but I say make the broad cook it. Cooking's woman's work."

"Easy to see why you're not married."

"I'm serious. I don't see why she should just get to lie around all day while we wait on her."

"She didn't exactly plan the party." Rio took a skillet from the dishes he'd washed earlier that morning. With roaches and who knows what other insects and rodents scampering about, detergent and hot water seemed a good idea. He placed the bacon in it and put it over a low fire, then started spreading butter on bread for toast.

Soft footfalls sounded in the hall. He turned around just as Jaime stepped inside the kitchen door.

"There's coffee," Rio said, his eyes riveted to the petite, but shapely woman who showed little signs of the stress she had to be feeling.

Her wraparound dress was wrinkled, but hugged her perky breasts and firm, round buttocks provocatively. She'd shed the jewelry and the sexy heels. Her bare feet and freshly scrubbed face made her look almost waif-like. Her hair, which had been up last night, was down, the strawberry-blond locks tumbling around her shoulders. Disheveled. Tempting.

"I'd like to take a shower," she said. "Or isn't there one in this disgusting place?"

"There's one," Rio said, "but it's not working. The water's a bit cold in the lake, but I'll walk you down there after breakfast if you'd like to bathe."

Luke leered at her. "I'll take care of that chore."

She shot him a castrating look. "I'd sooner wallow in mud."

"Yeah, that sounds fun, too."

Rio filled a clean mug with coffee and handed it to her. "There's sugar on the counter and milk in the fridge if you want it."

"No, this is fine," she murmured. "Thanks."

There was a pause before the last word, as if it was added as an afterthought. He hoped that meant she was coming around to the point where she might cooperate with him, but he wouldn't hold his breath waiting for that.

"How do you like your eggs?" he asked.

"Why ask her?" Luke quipped. "She ought to be cooking for us, if the princess knows how to scramble an egg."

Jaime marched across the kitchen, planted herself in front of the grease-stained range and grabbed the carton of eggs. She broke two into the small skillet and then glared at Luke. "How much arsenic do you want in yours?"

"You got a smart mouth on you, you know that? I want them over easy, and don't break the yolks."

Rio removed a pan of toast from beneath the broiler and watched as she deliberately pricked the first yolk and let the yellow run to the edges of the skillet. If they made it through breakfast without a major flare-up between her and Luke he'd be surprised—and relieved.

He didn't put anything beyond Luke, especially if

Jaime pushed him. He'd as soon rape her as not. The way he was looking at her right now evidenced the thought was already festering in his mind.

When the eggs were ready, Jaime slid them onto a plate, sprinkled them generously with salt and pepper and then tossed a couple of slices of toast next to them. "Jelly?" she asked, eyeing a large jar of strawberry preserves.

"Sure, sweetheart. Why not?" Luke said, smiling. "And I want you to sit with me while I eat. Right here," he said, patting his right knee. "We need to get to know each other better."

Her expression was one of fury, but her hands were steady as she opened the jar and spooned a large helping of the sticky condiment onto the plate next to the eggs. Padding across the floor determinedly, she stopped inches from Luke.

Luke patted his knee again. Jaime smiled. Rio's muscles hardened into bulging knots as he braced himself for trouble. Jaime took the last step and then tripped, falling against the table as the plate dropped from her hands and landed upside down in Luke's lap.

Curses flew from Luke's mouth as he leapt from the chair and grabbed her arm. "You bitch. You did that on purpose."

She tilted her head back and stared at him defiantly.

Luke fit one hand around her smooth neck, letting his fingers dig into the flesh. "Lick it off," he demanded. "Every drop. Lick it off." He pushed her face into the sugary mound of red preserves that clung to his jeans.

Jaime's knee jerked upward, connecting with Luke's groin, and this time the man went totally berserk. Rio flew across the room, reaching them just in time to stop Luke's fist before it slammed into Jaime's jaw.

He shoved Luke against the wall. "What the hell do you think you're doing?"

"Giving that tramp what she deserves. You saw what she did."

"That tramp is the reason we're here. Mess her up and you'll answer to Poncho. We both will. Is that what you want?"

"Poncho or not, I'm not taking that off no woman."

"She dropped a plate. That's all."

Luke muttered a new string of curses. "She didn't drop it. She dumped it on me."

"So get over it. We got a job to do and it doesn't include roughing up the victim. You could get carried away and blow the whole ransom deal. You know what that will get you."

The fight slowly went out of Luke. His muscles quit straining and his fists relaxed. By the time Rio let go of him, smoke was filling the room. Rio hurried to turn off the fire under the skillet.

And then he noticed that Jaime was nowhere in sight. Damn. In that split second when he was dealing with Luke, she must have made a getaway. But she was barefoot. She couldn't have gotten far.

He rushed toward the back door and caught sight of a wave of blue fabric weaving through the trees. He took off running, the pine straw skidding from beneath his feet, low limbs from scraggly trees tearing at his shirt.

If she escaped, he could kiss goodbye any chance of continuing to be a player. He made a dive for her as she skirted the muddy banks of the lake. They both went down in a tangle of arms, legs and wild locks of blond hair.

Jaime lay beneath him, facedown and spewing clumps of damp earth from her mouth. He rolled her to her back, straddled her and pinned her hands above her head to keep her from fighting him.

Her dress hung off one shoulder, revealing a mound of perfect flesh and a deep reddish-pink nipple that stared him in the face.

His body hardened and desire engulfed him in blistering waves. He rolled off her, leaving her short dress to bunch at her waist. A few wayward blond hairs peeked from beneath the wisp of black lace pantie.

He groaned, but kept her pinned to the earth. A man could only take so much.

Chapter Four

Jaime's heart pounded and her breath came in painful gasps.

"You're not making this easy," Rio said, staring into her eyes, his voice suddenly hoarse.

"Don't," she whispered. "Please, don't."

"I won't hurt you."

His words were all but drowned out by the sound of someone running in their direction. Luke. He'd been slower than Rio, but he was mere steps away now.

Rio let go of one of her arms and quickly tugged the shoulder of her dress back into place so that it covered her breast, his thumb brushing the tip of her nipple as he did. His muscles seemed to tense at the touch, but he didn't linger. By the time Luke reached them, he'd pulled her skirt back in place so that she was completely covered.

"I see you found the runaway princess," Luke said, his breathing still heavy as he almost stumbled over them.

"No thanks to you," Rio snapped.

Luke's face twisted into a scowl. "Don't go laying the blame on me. She'd have never escaped in the first place if you hadn't been acting like some macho hero."

"I've just got better sense than to damage the merchandise before we're paid for it."

Luke spit in the dirt, the phlegm falling mere inches from Jaime's head. Her stomach turned, but this time she bit back the angered sarcasm that flew to her tongue.

She had to play this smarter. Angering Luke wasn't going to speed her escape or help her stay alive until her brothers could rescue her.

"Go back to the house," Rio ordered. "I've got unfinished business with the princess."

"You're not my boss."

"Damn good thing."

"And you don't own the woman."

Rio laid a hand on Jaime possessively, his thumbs resting just below her breasts. Luke lingered, staring at her as if he could see right through the wrinkled dress before leering contemptuously and ambling back toward the house.

Rio's gaze followed Luke until he'd completely disappeared in the trees. He exhaled slowly and scooted away from Jaime, letting go of her entirely.

"I can't say much for the company you keep," Jaime said.

"I didn't do the choosing."

"You're here."

"I do what I have to."

"Then just let me go," she pleaded. "I'll pay you and you won't have to split the ransom with anyone."

"It doesn't work that way."

"It could." But it was clear he wasn't buying and what he did say didn't make a lot of sense. "How much ransom did you ask for?"

"Can't say."

"Because you let those stupid thugs call all the shots?"

"For now, except with you. I'll be calling the shots with you, and if you've got a brain in that pretty little head of yours, you'll listen. Rule number one, don't try anything stupid like that feeble escape attempt again."

Not until she got half a chance.

Rio moved into a sitting position and tugged her up to do the same. "We need to talk, Jaime."

"I've told you all I plan to about my brothers. You may collect a ransom, but you'll never live to enjoy it. They'll hunt you down and—"

"I know about your siblings. Your oldest brother Langston is CEO of Collingsworth Oil. Your brothers Matt and Bart run Jack's Bluff Ranch. Your brother Zach is in law enforcement. Your sister, Becky, is married to Nick Ridgely, former Dallas Cowboy star."

Just as she expected. The kidnappers knew her situation all too well. She hadn't been a random hit.

"Who's the black sheep of the family?" Rio asked.

"We don't have one. We leave the dirty dealings to people like you."

"Every family has a backslider, maybe one who's

involved with dealing drugs. That pays really well these days, I'm told. A huge, respectable ranch might be just the place to stash a shipment from Mexico."

Fury fired through her. One minute she could almost convince herself to trust Rio. The next, she ached to slap him hard across that rugged, handsome face. "How dare you accuse my brothers of something so despicable!"

"I'm just asking."

"I'm through talking to you." She stood, yanking her dress down to cover as much thigh as she could. "Now I'm going to walk down to that lake and wash the mud off me. You do as you please."

He smiled for the first time since he'd tackled her to the ground. "Is that an invitation?"

For some stupid reason, she felt heat rush to her cheeks. She turned so Rio wouldn't see her blush.

"You don't need an invitation. You have the gun. But don't think I'd ever welcome your touch, not if you were the only man left on earth." She stamped away without looking back.

She could hear Rio following her, and turned when she reached the water's edge. He'd stopped a few yards from her and leaned against a tree, giving her space. He looked relaxed, cocky. More like a sexy protector than a villain who held her life in his hands.

Probably all part of his diabolical plan, she told herself. He expected her to trust him because he didn't force himself on her and protected her from Luke's perverted advances. She had to find a way to escape, but outsmarting Rio might be impossible.

That left Luke. He was totally disgusting and she wouldn't put anything past him. But it was clear he was the weaker of the two both mentally and physically. If she was going to escape, it would have to be on his watch.

Heaven help her if she failed and was left at his mercy alone.

ZACH ARRIVED BACK at the hospital at ten before ten in the morning, parked in a space reserved for law enforcement and bolted up the stairs to the ICU waiting room where he and his brothers and sister were to meet with the doctor.

Langston, Bart and Becky had been there since they'd followed the ambulance to the hospital last night. Matt had stayed at the big house in case there was a call from the kidnappers. So far there hadn't been.

Zach had been on the move, investigating the crime scene on his own and combing police records for cons who met the descriptions Buerto had given them. He was no closer to a lead on who had abducted Jaime.

Langston saw Zach enter the waiting room and motioned him to the far left corner of the room where they'd staked claim to a group of chairs. "The doctor's with Mother now. He'll see us as soon as he comes out."

"Glad I made it in time. Have you seen Mom since we last talked?"

"They let me go in for a couple of minutes," Becky

said. "The nurse thought I might calm her." Her voice lowered. "Even drugged, she's restless and jerky, and there was nothing I could say to change that."

Zach leaned forward and rested his elbows on his knees. "Did she ask about Jaime?"

"No. She's still drifting in and out of sleep from the drugs they're giving her, but the nurse said she'd called out Jaime's name when she was sleeping. I'm sure that as soon as she's fully alert, she'll demand answers."

Zach wished to hell they had some. "As soon as the doctor finishes with us, we have to find a place to talk in private."

Bart nodded. "I'm for that. I think we should reconsider our current strategy."

They'd agreed to hold off on calling in the cops or the FBI until they heard the kidnappers' demands, but no one had expected the wait to be this long.

Zach's phone rang. The group grew instantly quiet, though there was no real reason to think the kidnappers had his cell number. He answered.

"Buerto," he said out loud, so that they would know to whom he was talking. They stared at him, their anxiety tangible.

"I've heard from the kidnappers," Buerto said.

"Why did they call you?"

"I guess because I was with her when they abducted her."

"What did they say?"

"It would be better if we could talk about this in person."

"I'm at the hospital waiting to talk to Mom's cardiologist."

"I'm already on my way to the ranch, so I can be at the hospital in about fifteen minutes, twenty at the most."

"I don't see the point in waiting that long."

"Can you talk freely?"

"I can listen."

"Not good enough. The deal they want is complicated."

Zach's irritation level skyrocketed. The kidnappers should have come directly to the family. Where did they get off dealing with some guy who was a stranger to all of them?

"Call me the second you arrive at the hospital."

"Naturally," Buerto answered and then quickly broke the connection. Zach returned his phone to the clip at his waist.

"Contact?" Langston asked, carefully choosing his words so that no one outside the family would know they were talking about a kidnapping.

"Yeah. Through Buerto. He's on his way here right now."

"Why call him?" Becky asked, her question echoing his own. "He's not family."

Doctor Gathrite joined them before Zach was forced to admit he had no answer to that question.

"There's a small conference room down the hall we can use," the doctor said. "It will be more private there."

They followed him to a room that smelled of stale coffee. The furniture was limited to a half dozen metal folding chairs and a table barely big enough for the five of them to squeeze around. A counter on the back wall held a coffee maker that had long since finished brewing.

Dr. Gathrite stood back for them to enter, then offered coffee, which only Langston accepted. The cardiologist settled in a chair at the head of the table.

Zach found a spot to stand against the side wall. He was too keyed up to sit.

"Do you have the results of the tests, Doctor?" Becky asked.

"We do, at least enough to make a few diagnostic assessments. The good news is there's no significant blockage in the arteries that feed the heart and no sign of a blood clot."

"I don't understand," Bart said. "If there's no blockage, what caused the coronary attack?"

"The attack appears to have been caused by a sudden spasm, one so intense that it cut off the blood flow through the artery. That's far less common than an attack brought on by cardiovascular disease or a clot, but it sometimes happens in otherwise heart-healthy individuals."

Langston set his coffee cup on the table in front of him. "Then you think her heart attack was brought on by stress?"

"There are factors other than emotional or physical trauma that can cause a spasm, such as certain drugs or exposure to extreme weather conditions. But, yes, in your mother's case, the evidence points to stress."

Becky clasped her hands in front of her. "How much damage was there to her heart?"

"You can count your blessings there, too," Dr. Gathrite said. "The permanent damage is minimal. The issue now is having her avoid any additional emotional trauma."

Which was basically impossible unless they were able to arrange Jaime's safe return quickly. Zach only half listened to the rest of the doctor's spiel and the details of treatment. Zach's concern for his mother was a given, but the only way he could help her, or Jaime, was to acquire Jaime's safe release.

His cell phone vibrated and he checked the caller ID. Buerto. Zach excused himself and went into the hall to take the call.

Langston followed him. "This is a family dilemma, Zach. Bart, Matt and I will be with you when you meet with Buerto."

He clapped his oldest brother on the back. "I never doubted for a minute that you would."

IT WAS LATE AFTERNOON BEFORE Jaime heard from either of her kidnappers again, though she could hear them talking through the thin walls. Occasionally she heard a door slam or Luke's snorting laugh.

She'd tried her door a couple of times, but it was locked tight. And the boards that had been nailed over the window wouldn't budge. She'd need something on the order of a pickax to remove them. If she ever got outside this room again, she'd snoop to see what kind of tools she could find.

Finally, Rio opened the door and ordered her out to eat. She followed him to the kitchen. Luke lay on the sofa, his bare feet hanging over the edge. His gun was on a homemade coffee table instead of tucked inside his shoulder holster. It was the only good sign.

"I made you a sandwich," Rio said, pushing a plate toward her. "It's not much, but it will keep you going."

She washed her hands at the kitchen sink and returned to the table, choosing a chair that made it easy to watch Luke and the gun. It was almost as if he were taunting her with it, deliberately tempting her to steal it.

The sandwich was a couple of slices of white bread smeared with a spicy mustard and wrapped around a piece of tasteless luncheon meat. She chewed and choked it down with a sip of lukewarm bottled water.

The two men barely spoke to each other as she ate, but when they did, the growing tension between them crackled like flames in a pile of dry leaves. Had she caused or merely added to the friction? She suspected it was the latter.

Luke looked disgustingly disheveled, his clothes wrinkled and stained from the breakfast she'd dumped in his lap. The underarms of his shirt were circled with perspiration. A glob of what looked to be dried mustard stuck to the stubble of whiskers on his chin.

Rio, on the other hand, had apparently bathed in the lake. His hair was damp, raked back but with thick locks falling over his forehead. He was shirtless, revealing a muscled six-pack, a rock-hard abdomen. He wore his virility well.

Luke rose, padded past her and stopped at the back door, staring out like a caged animal. "I need some whiskey."

Rio ignored the comment.

"I'm serious, man. I need a drink."

"There's water."

Luke uttered a string of vile curses, then walked back to the sofa and plopped down on the saggy, soiled cushions. "We got a car right outside. It wouldn't hurt anything for me to drive into the nearest town and find a liquor store."

"You have a short memory. Poncho said the car was to be used only at his orders. I didn't hear him order a whiskey run."

"Well, if I have to stay cooped up in this godforsaken place much longer without liquor, I'll go nuts. How's that for a friggin' emergency?"

"Suck it up," Rio said.

"Suck it up yourself, pantywaist. I got the key to that car right here." He pulled a metal ring from his pocket and shook it. "You think you can stop me if I decide to take the vehicle?"

Rio stood and glared down at Luke, his muscles flexed so that his forearms looked like balls of steel. "I could stop you if I gave a damn. I don't. If you want to flout Poncho's rules, go right ahead. In the meantime, I suggest you guard the prisoner." With that he turned and strode out the back door, leaving her alone with Luke.

Jaime pushed the rest of her sandwich aside and walked to the back door. Rio trod the path to the lake, and then stepped into a cluster of trees, disappearing from sight. A sliver of panic rode her spine—an unconscious, but stupid and dangerous reaction. If she started depending on Rio to save her, she was doomed.

She was alone with Luke now. He had the car key and a weapon resting beside him in plain sight. If she could get her hands on the key and the gun, the power would switch to her hands.

Her heart began to race as a plan took form. She smoothed her hair with her fingers and bit her lips to give them some color. There was nothing she could do about her bare feet or the less than pristine condition of her dress.

Retaking her seat and turning toward Luke, she crossed her legs and kicked one seductively. "How do you stand Rio bossing you around all the time?"

Luke looked her up and down, leering as his gaze settled on various parts of her body. She struggled to keep from retching.

"What's the matter?" he asked. "Did the macho Navy SEAL go limp on you this morning?"

"Rio's a SEAL?" She blurted out the question without thinking.

"He was until they kicked him out. I'm surprised he didn't tell you. He thinks it makes him better than me."

It wouldn't take much to be better than Luke. Still, it shocked Jaime to think that a former SEAL could be mixed up in a kidnapping at gunpoint.

"I think you should go get that whiskey," she said. "I know I could use some."

"Sure, go get the whiskey and leave you alone so you can try to escape again."

"You could take me with you."

"And have you yell out in the store that I'm holding you captive? I'm nobody's fool, princess."

"I never said you were." She walked over and sat down beside him. He smelled of garlic and sweat, making her stomach churn.

He laid a hand on her thigh. "Now you're getting smart, sweetheart. I'm the real man here. You be good to me, and I'll be good to you."

"How good?" She forced a sultry tone to her voice and fought off another wave of nausea. The impulse to stare at the gun was almost overpowering, but she couldn't do anything to make Luke suspicious.

He pressed his lips against hers. Fighting revulsion and the urge to clock him, she kissed him back. When his hands groped beneath her dress, she reached out and closed her hand around the gun.

"Hands over your head or I'll shoot," she ordered as she broke the kiss.

Curses fired from Luke's mouth, but he raised his hands above his head. She took a deep breath, working to get her wits about her. Then with one quick move,

Luke battered his head into her chest. She fell backward, but didn't let go of the gun.

Her finger circled the trigger, but before she could pull it, Luke kicked the pistol from her hands. She fell on top of it, but he yanked her back up by her hair. The pain was so intense, she felt as if she were being scalped. She kept fighting for the gun, but Luke was too strong for her. The weapon slipped from her grasp.

She tried to break away and run. Her foot slipped.

Gunfire exploded in her brain and blood splattered over her like crimson rain.

Chapter Five

"Lawmen are reporting lots of new faces in Texas border towns."

"Assassins?"

"It's possible, but not definite. No one has come up with details, but the consensus is that Detonation Day is imminent. We may have a matter of days to stop it. Perhaps less."

And Rio was stuck out here in this miserable cabin guarding some woman the drug lords had decided was worth kidnapping. "I've let everybody down," he said into his miniature cell phone.

"If you go strictly by results, we all have. As long as you're in the middle of the kidnapping, you may still be valuable. And if not, you're in a position to save at least one—"

A thunderous clap of gunfire drowned out the rest of the sentence. Rio took off running without bothering to explain. He covered the few yards to the cabin in seconds, horror building at what he might find.

The blood was the first image that registered when he opened the door. It dripped from Jaime's face and puddled in the folds of her dress. She'd fallen back against the cushions of the sofa. Her eyes were glazed with dread—or pain.

He plunged back into the past and into a memory so vivid that sharp pains needled his heart. He had trouble breathing. His feet refused to move.

A split second later, adrenaline coursed through his veins again, and he crossed the space that separated him from Jaime. It was then that he spotted Luke, draped over the far side of the sofa, still clutching the pistol though his left leg was soaked in blood. The leg of his jeans was torn from the bullet and Luke was using his left hand to apply pressure to the gaping wound.

"The bitch shot me."

It was Luke who'd been shot, not Jaime. The blood was Luke's. Rio had little success wrapping his mind around how that had happened but it was enough for now that she was okay.

Luke raised the pistol and pointed it at Jaime. "No woman shoots me and gets away with it."

Rio extended his open hand. "Give me the gun, Luke."

"Get the hell out of my way or I swear I'll kill you, too."

"You kill Jaime, and Poncho will see that you never see another sunrise. Is a death sentence what you want, Luke? If not, hand me the damn pistol."

Luke muttered under his breath, a few curses that

even Rio hadn't heard before, but he had to know Rio had spoken the truth.

"Just hand me the gun so I can treat the wound."

Luke grimaced and fell back to the couch, finally dropping the gun to the floor.

Rio kicked it to the other side of the room and turned to Jaime. "Are you okay?"

She nodded. "I didn't shoot him. I took the gun from him but he wrestled it away from me. He was holding it when it went off."

"We'll sort it out later."

"That's how it happened."

"I believe you."

Not that the details mattered. For Rio, knowing she was okay stilled the panic that had nearly torn him apart when he'd first heard the gunshot and again when he'd seen the blood.

He took her hand and squeezed it. The touch vibrated through him and he dropped her hand too quickly, backing away from her and turning toward Luke before he had time to think about why she affected him the way she did.

He put a hand on Luke's shoulder. "I should take a look at that wound."

"If you can drag yourself away from the bitch that long."

Jaime stood a bit shakily. "I'll wash up in case you need help with Luke."

Luke glared at her. "You lay a hand on me, and I'll break it off."

"Go back to the bedroom," Rio said, trying to calm the wounded man and make this easier on Jaime. "If I need you, I'll call for you."

She nodded and walked away, shoulders squared, head high in spite of what she'd been through. Jaime was all woman, but she had a fighting spirit about her that would have fit in well with his team of frogmen.

Rio knelt next to Luke. "You'll have to move that hand if you want me to take a look at your wound."

"If I do, the blood may start gushing again."

"If it does, I'll make a tourniquet and call an ambulance."

"Are you crazy? No way am I going to a hospital. They'll ask questions and call the cops. You know how Poncho feels about cop trouble."

Luke released the pressure slowly. Blood oozed from the wound, and Luke made a gagging sound at the sight of the exposed muscle and tissue.

"The bullet's imbedded. It will have to come out," Rio said.

"So do it," Luke said. "And then I'm gonna really need that whiskey."

"We don't even have basic first-aid supplies. There's no way I can treat this kind of injury. You need a doctor."

"Then call Poncho. Tell him his slutty piece of collateral shot me. He'll tell you what to do."

"I warned you to stay away from Jaime," Rio said. "Guess you should have listened to me for a change."

"Go to hell."

"Are you sure you don't want me to call an ambulance?"

"No. Call Poncho."

Rio put in the call, left a message and then found a clean cloth to bandage the open wound while he waited ten minutes for Poncho to call him back. As he expected, Poncho went verbally ballistic at the news.

"I trusted you to handle the situation, Rio," he yelled.

"I wasn't the one who let the woman take my gun away from me."

Poncho let out a disgusted breath. "How bad is he hurt?"

"The bleeding has slowed, but the bullet will have to be removed or risk major infection. And he'll want something for the pain."

"Damn. We don't need this, not now."

"Bad timing," Rio agreed. "How are the ransom negotiations going?"

"Her brothers want proof she's alive and well before they concede to anything, but they'll come though. If not, I'll send her home in pieces. I'm setting up a call between you and them. I'll be on the line as well. Any funny stuff and I break the connection at once."

"What makes you think they won't trace the call?"

"The calls will be initiated from a virtually untraceable phone to the virtually untraceable phone you have. The FBI or CIA might be able to trace it if we made repeated calls. We won't. Besides, they haven't contacted the FBI."

"What makes you so sure?"

"They want Jaime back alive."

"When were you going to give me those details?"

"I was working them out when you called."

"Anything else going on I should know about?" Like the whole border about to go up in smoke? Rio thought.

"You just take care of the business at hand without any more trouble."

"Keep it straight, Poncho. I didn't foul up. Luke did."

"Just try to keep him alive until I can get someone out there to pick him up. It may be morning before I can replace him so you'll be alone with Jaime tonight. Make certain she doesn't escape—or shoot you." He added a few expletives to illustrate his irritation.

"One more thing, Rio. I don't want Jaime on the phone with her brother for more than a minute or two. Convince her that if she says anything other than that she's alive and well, she'll never see her family or her lover again."

"I'll take care of it." His way, not Poncho's.

So the Collingsworths were capitulating. After what he'd heard about them, he'd almost expected a fight. He still wouldn't rule that out, not if they were half as fiery as Jaime.

And with every second Rio was guarding her, he was running out of time to make a difference in a plot that might leave thousands of innocent people dead.

Rio had no choice but to change the game plan.

JAIME TREMBLED AS SHE CLOSED the bathroom door and stepped out of the blood-drenched dress and sticky panties. This nightmare was really starting to get to her. She hadn't shot Luke, but that didn't mean he didn't have it coming. He was a rotten pervert and he'd have shot her if Rio hadn't shown up when he did.

Picking up the thin, worn washcloth Rio had given her, she soaped it thoroughly and started scrubbing her face. She'd never felt so unclean in her life, not even when she'd been thrown from her horse into a mud pit last year. It wasn't just the blood that was sickening. It was everything about this moldy cabin and the fact that Luke had actually laid his grubby paws on her.

Her life had turned into a living hell. Rio was the one exception and a major conundrum. She should abhor his touch the same as she did Luke's, but in truth, weird and inexplicable things happened to her equilibrium when he got close.

It wasn't just his rugged good looks or his cocky swagger. She was fickle, not shallow. It wasn't even the way he mesmerized her with his piercing gaze or the way he took charge of every situation. It was a prevailing and inexplicable feeling that he really was on her side.

She scrubbed harder, rubbing the skin on her arms and body until it was red and prickly. All the while she struggled to get a handle on Rio. She'd felt his need for her today when he'd wrestled her to the ground. She'd seen the desire in his eyes. Yet he hadn't made a move on her.

And then there was the way he'd looked at her when he'd come running into the cabin at the sound of gunfire.

The anxiety that had tightened every line of his face had ebbed the second he'd realized that she hadn't been shot.

Luke had the essence of evil all about him. Rio didn't. Yet he was in on the kidnapping. She couldn't trust him, couldn't let him play her. She'd have to keep her guard up every second they were together. This time she couldn't rely on intuition.

When she'd scrubbed and rinsed every inch of her body, she washed her hair with the coarse soap and rinsed it as best she could beneath the low faucet. Finally, she felt reasonably clean, but the only thing she had to put on was the soiled dress.

God, would she love to step into her own closet and wrap herself in one of the silks, cottons or buttery knits. And she'd all but kill for her flowery fragranced body cream to massage into her skin. If she got out of this alive, she'd never take any luxury for granted again.

Whoa. This was no time to think of fatal ifs. She was a Collingsworth. They didn't give up just because things got tough.

Still, she jumped at a tap on her door. It had to be Rio, though there was nothing to keep him from just barging in on her. She wrapped her hair in the towel and grabbed the top sheet, jerking it from the bed and wrapping it around her sarong style.

She took what she considered a formidable stance, arms folded to hold the sheet firmly in place. "Come in."

He opened the door and took a few steps inside, letting in the late afternoon sunshine that had filtered through the cabin's windows. His gaze scanned her slowly, but his expression never changed.

"You cleaned up already," he said. "I was going to see if you wanted to walk down to the lake and bathe."

"And make it convenient for you to drown me for trying to steal Luke's gun?"

He cocked his head and raked a wayward lock of dark hair from his forehead. "After seeing Luke, I'd be scared you'd drown me."

"How is Luke?"

"He'll live, but he needs medical attention. Someone is coming to pick him up and take him to a doctor."

So Luke would be leaving. She'd be alone with Rio. An edgy nervousness jumped along her nerves, not totally unlike the buzz she got skiing down a formidable slope or riding her Harley on a narrow mountain road.

"I have other news," Rio said.

"About Luke?"

"No. I'm expecting a phone call from your family any minute, Jaime. They want to know that you're alive and well before they meet the ransom demands."

Her heart skipped a few beats. She was actually going to talk to someone in her family. Unfortunately, she couldn't give them a clue as to how to rescue her since she didn't know where she was other than on a lake. She'd been so disoriented from the drugs they'd injected her with that nothing had registered between the time they left her neighborhood and the time they arrived at the isolated cabin.

"What is the ransom?" she asked.

"I don't know. I need you to find that out from your brother."

"And then what? You'll ask for double that to let me escape?"

"You don't give an inch, do you, Jaime Collings-worth?" The expression on his face grew tight. His muscles clenched.

"Hit me," she taunted. "Go ahead if that will make you feel more like a man."

"I'm not going to hit you," he said, his eyes darkening with a multitude of emotions. Anger, frustration…and was that desire she saw in their depths? He stepped closer. "Though I can see how you could drive a man to—" He stopped, and she felt the air between them sizzle.

"To what, Rio?"

He looked at her for a moment, then shook his head. "Forget it."

His cell phone rang. He took the call, responded with a couple of affirmatives, and then put the phone on speaker. "It's Buerto."

The mention of his name shook her and made her feel a tad guilty. He'd fought to save her and then she'd all but forgotten about him with all that was going on.

"Jaime, you can't imagine how good it is to hear your voice. I've been berating myself constantly that I couldn't save you."

"It was one against three, Buerto."

"Still, a man should be able to protect his woman. Have they hurt you? Have the pigs violated you?"

"No." *Thanks to Rio,* she thought. "Have you talked to my family, Buerto?"

"Yes, of course. Zach is standing beside me now. They told us we only had a couple of minutes when they put us through to you, but I had to hear for myself you were fine. You know how much you mean to me. I can't bear thinking of you with those monsters."

"Thanks. Can I talk to Zach now?"

"How are you, sis?"

The slight tremor she heard in his voice told her just how worried he was and brought tears to her eyes. "I'm fine, but I miss you guys. How's Mom?"

The silence lasted too long. Panic swelled into a choking knot in her throat. "She's taking this hard, isn't she?"

"She'll be great the minute you walk in the front door of the big house and she hears you laugh." He paused a moment. "We're negotiating with the kidnappers, Jaime. We'll get you home safely even if we have to move mountains."

"I never doubted it, Zach. I'll just stay in this isolated lake cabin and wait until you do."

Rio put his hand on her shoulder, a threat firing in his dark eyes, a warning that she was saying too much. "I have no idea where I am," she added quickly before they took the phone from her, "but they're treating me well."

"Buerto's been a big help," Zach said. "The kidnappers are using him as the go-between. He negotiated this call."

So that's why Buerto was in on this. The kidnappers were using him.

Rio's grip tightened on her shoulder. "Time's about up."

And she hadn't asked the question he wanted answered. Tough. Only the answer affected her, too. "Zach, what is the ransom?"

"Two million in cash and we're to fly some cargo into Mexico for them in…"

Dead silence replaced his worried voice.

"Zach? Zach, are you still there?"

The connection had been broken. Her time had apparently run out.

Rio shoved the phone back into his pocket. "I need to know what cargo they're shipping and the details of the flight. Time. Locations."

"I wasn't the one who broke the connection," she reminded him.

"We'll have other options—as soon as Luke is out of here."

The intensity in his voice was alarming. She was almost certain it had nothing to do with her. "What's this really about, Rio?"

"Lives, Jaime. Lots of innocent lives could be on the line." He kept his voice low so there was no chance Luke could overhear him. "Better sit down. What I need to tell you may sound a bit far-fetched."

Chapter Six

Telling Jaime the truth about his involvement with the CIA and Homeland Security was risky at best, but allowing that cargo to ship could be disastrous. She was smart and intuitive. He'd have to give this to her straight and count on her to cooperate.

He sat down next to her on the bed. "I'm not who you think I am, Jaime. I'm an undercover agent working for the CIA and Homeland Security on a covert operation to stop what we think may be a deadly terrorist attack on America's southern border."

She inched away from him, her expression marked by suspicion. "And you kidnapped me because you think I have terrorist ties? That's absurd."

"I didn't plan the kidnapping. I didn't even know about it until a few minutes before we drove up at your house. Even then, I told you to trust me."

"You didn't know what was going on and yet you showed up with luggage. You were able to change into clean clothes."

"I was told to bring a bag." He raked a hand through his hair. "Look, I know you have no reason to believe me, but give me a chance. I'm trying to keep you safe along with everything else."

"If you couldn't stop the kidnapping, I don't see how you can ensure my safety. Had you run in the back door a split second later this afternoon, Luke would have killed me."

As if he needed a reminder of that. "If you'd trusted me as I'd asked, you wouldn't have tried to steal his gun and the shooting wouldn't have happened," he reminded her.

Her eyes narrowed. "Why would the government hire a Navy SEAL who'd been dishonorably discharged to work undercover?"

"I was discharged, but not dishonorably. That lie was created to get me inside the workings of one of the major Mexican drug cartels. It worked. I moved through the ranks quickly, but not quickly enough. Obviously they still don't trust me fully or I'd have had prior knowledge concerning your abduction."

"And now you think that my kidnapping is connected to an attack that the drug cartels are planning?"

He nodded. "I didn't at first, but I do after hearing your conversation with Zach. The drug cartels have enough money to buy a small planet, but their every move in this country is being monitored right now. They've had numerous shipments of drugs coming into the country and arms going out of the country seized by border patrol agents and the CIA."

Jaime stood. The sheet she was wearing caught on a bedspring, tugging it so that her right breast was exposed almost to the nipple. She yanked it back in place as his senses reeled.

Faced with the gravity of the situation, he shouldn't even be noticing that she was a woman, much less having sensual surges so intense they made his head spin. But Jaime was not just any woman. She was incredibly sexy. Spunky as hell. And smart enough that she was weighing everything he said.

He turned away as she started to pace the small room. Even draped in a yellowed sheet, the gentle sway of her hips was a turn-on.

She stopped and stared him down. "You kidnap me, hold me hostage, and now you expect me to believe some wild story you've concocted about terrorists and covert operations?"

"I know how it sounds, but I'm telling you the truth, Jaime. The CIA has intercepted and partially deciphered messages that talk of an imminent Detonation Day and a payback that border law enforcement will never forget."

"And if my family goes through with the ransom demands they might not only be helping fund their dirty work but smuggling in goods that they'll need in that attack."

"That's how it looks to me."

"Are you talking about illegal arms deals?"

"The real fear is it could be worse."

"Something more deadly, like chemicals?"

He nodded. "That's a possibility. And the cartel knows that it's highly unlikely that a Collingsworth Oil flight would attract the attention of authorities. You're not only wealthy and influential, but you have a history of lawful business dealings. You were fully invested a couple years back."

"How do you know so much about my family?"

"I made a phone call to Cutter Martin."

She spun around and walked back to where he was still sitting on the bed. "Are you talking about Cutter Martin of Dobbin, Texas?"

"Yeah."

"How do you know Cutter?"

"We met when we were both SEALs. He recruited me to work for his Double M Investigative and Protective Service. He had a contract with Homeland Security and I was dropped into this assignment."

She wrapped her hands around the bedpost and rested her towel-wrapped head against the spindly column. "Is your name even Rio?"

He nodded. "Rio Hernandez. Texas born and raised, on a ranch out in El Paso."

She let her gaze meet his and hold. A drop of water escaped a curl that was peeking out from beneath the towel. It rolled down her cheek. He wiped it away with the tip of his thumb and his awareness surged to the danger level.

"Your wife must hate that you left the SEALs only to take on another job that puts your life in danger."

"My wife is dead." The words pealed like distant thunder, echoing through the recesses of his mind and awakening the hurt that had almost put him under at the time. He couldn't afford to get bogged down in that now. He had to focus on the present. Lives were at stake. He had to convince Jaime of that.

"You have to talk to Zach for me, Jaime. Time is of the essence. Cooperate with me on this and I'll see that you get home safely. That's a promise."

"When will I get home and how?"

"I don't have all that worked out yet, but as soon as we confiscate that shipment, I'll do everything I can to see that you get out of this alive."

"That's not much of a guarantee."

"I realize I don't have much to offer in the way of bargaining power. But I'm not asking you to do it for me. Do it for all the innocent men, women and children who'll die if we can't stop the attack."

"If I believed you, I'd have no choice but to agree."

"You don't have to take my word for it. I'll call Cutter and you can get him to vouch for me."

"I haven't seen Cutter in years. I have no real reason to trust him, either."

A banging at the door interrupted the discussion.

"Sounds as if Luke's ride has arrived," Rio said. "I'll help get him in the car, but think about what I said. I need you with me on this. Without you, we're running on empty."

"I'll think about it."

She brushed his arm with her hand and a current shot from his head to his groin. He ground his teeth, steeled his resistance and walked away. Jaime was part of the mission and that was all she could ever be to him. His past and the vast differences between them dictated that.

THE CABIN FELT DIFFERENT with Luke no longer in it. Now it was only Jaime and Rio and a predicament that opened a new realm of deadly possibilities. If Rio was telling the truth, she might be able to help the CIA stop an attack that could leave hundreds or perhaps thousands dead. If he was lying, then he could be simply manipulating her for his own gain.

Her instincts all screamed that he was telling the truth, but that could be part and parcel of the sensual effect he had on her. She could no longer deny that she was physically attracted to him. When his dark eyes locked with hers, she felt both frightened and excited.

She had to find out if he was telling the truth. Talking to Cutter Martin wouldn't give her a definitive answer, but it would help. Her brother Langston and Cutter had been close friends years ago. He'd seemed like a decent guy.

Her pulse raced as Rio punched in Cutter's number. Rio talked for a few minutes, filling Cutter in on all that had happened within the last hour. The shooting. The phone call connecting her with Zach and Buerto.

She couldn't imagine that her strong-willed brothers liked having Buerto involved in the negotiations.

Evidently the kidnappers had given them no choice in the matter.

From the way Buerto had talked, it seemed he had read a lot more into their relationship than she had. Maybe that was the guilt talking since he hadn't been able to fight off the kidnappers.

Rio handed her the phone, but it wasn't the one he'd used earlier. This one was a quarter the size, so small it could be easily hidden in the palm of her hand. And this time it wasn't set to the speaker function.

Cutter, or at least a man claiming to be him, started talking the instant Rio handed her the phone. "Hi, Jaime. Cutter Martin here."

The voice sounded vaguely familiar, but she couldn't be sure. "It's been a while," she said.

"Years. You were just a kid back when Langston and I were competing against each other in bronc riding."

"I may have been young, but I was the best barrel rider in two counties."

"You were pretty good, as I remember."

"I was better than that." She still wasn't convinced about Cutter, so she continued. "Your aunt used to come and watch you ride but then she'd just sit up in the stands and read," she baited. "Everybody teased her about it."

"Aunt Merlee didn't read. She knitted. I think she made a baby sweater for every baby born in the tri-county area while watching me compete."

That was the kind of detail she needed to assure herself

she was talking to her brother's old friend. "Give me reasons I should trust Rio," she said. "What's going on?"

"He's telling you the truth. He's working through my investigative service, the Double M, for the CIA. We're working against the clock, Jaime. We know there will be a major attack, but unless we know how, when and where, we can't stop it."

"Do you agree that my kidnapping is part of it?"

"I hadn't thought of it until Rio brought it up, but the timing makes sense. There's no reason for the drug lords to risk an abduction of a prominent person like you days before a planned attack unless it is an essential aspect of their plan. That's why we need Zach to work with Rio to find out the what, when and where of the cargo shipment."

"Couldn't Zach just work with you?"

"It's more complicated than that. Rio's identity has to be guarded or you could both end up dead before we have a chance to intervene. It's better if I just stay out of this for now and Rio remains just one of the kidnappers."

"Zach is never going to trust a man holding me captive, no matter what I say to him."

"Don't underestimate him. He's in law enforcement. He has to know what we're dealing with along the Texas border right now. Payback killings against officers are commonplace. The cartels are literally taking over the towns and making it unsafe for the citizens to walk the streets."

"I'll do what I can."

"That's all we're asking. One more thing about Rio. The CIA specifically sought him out when they heard he was leaving the service and that he was coming to work with my team. That's why they falsified documents to make it look as if he was kicked out of the SEALs."

"Why him specifically?"

"His record of success and bravery is amazing. His risk-taking is legendary. He does what has to be done, consequences and conventional wisdom be dammed. That doesn't always fly well in the military. They frown on loose cannons, and Rio earned that label his first year."

"I'm not sure what that means for me, Cutter."

"Just that his ideas may seem to lack credence at times, but his instincts for figuring out the enemy are unrivaled. Trust him."

Trust Rio no matter how implausible his ideas. Cutter made it sound easy, but what if that trust was a mistake and Rio was really in league with the devils behind all of this? What if he was manipulating all of them to improve his position in the cartel or to milk even more money from her family?

She studied the hard, unrelenting lines in Rio's face and the exigency that swam in the intoxicating depths of his eyes. She realized it was too late for her questions. Whether or not she should trust Rio was a moot point.

She already did.

"Take care, Jaime. Rio will get you out of this alive. As for the rest of the innocent lives, they still hang in the balance."

She thanked Cutter for being so honest with her and broke the connection. Then she looked up at Rio. "Do you want me to make the call to Zach now?"

"Not yet. We need a strategy first. Your shoes are by the back door. Put them on and we'll take a walk down to the lake. Best not to go barefoot out there in the dark."

The sun had finished setting. Facing the muddy trail by the light of the moon in a toga and a pair of stiletto sandals was not her idea of fun. However, the thought of escaping the oppression of this stuffy cabin and stepping out into the cool night air overcame her objections. Not that Rio had asked for her approval.

She lifted the layers of sheet that tangled around her ankles and followed Rio from the bedroom prison. Her shoes were waiting just as Rio had said. Only they'd been butchered. The beautiful heels had been cut off, leaving the edges ragged and hideously unattractive.

She stooped and picked them up, cradling them as she fought a new wave of frustration. "You ruined my shoes. How could you?"

"Easy. I just picked up that butcher knife over there and whacked them."

Her hands flew to her hips. "Don't ever touch my shoes again."

"You can play fashion queen on your own time. Escaping through the woods in those would be suicide— just in case it comes to that. You can thank me later."

But those sandals were brand-new and absolutely stunning. Any woman would know that. "You—you—

you loose cannon," she muttered, for want of a better retort.

He smiled and opened the door for her. "Don't start buttering me up so soon. You ain't seen nothin' yet."

"YOU LOOK LIKE YOU GOT ONE wheel down and the axle dragging."

Lenora opened her eyes at the sound of Billy Mack's voice. "About time you got here." Her words stalled on her thick tongue. The heart attack and the medication were taking their toll.

"I didn't expect you to miss me so much you'd be asking for me this soon."

"I don't. I *need* you."

"Sure didn't expect you to admit that. Aren't they treating you well around here?"

She gathered her thoughts from the mire of confusion created by the drugs. "It's about Jaime."

"I was sure it would be." He put his mouth close to her ear. "I can't go there with you, Lenora, not in here. There are too many ears to hear the conversation."

"Then they told you?"

Billy Mack nodded. She'd thought they surely would. He'd been their neighbor for so long he was like family now. He'd become a proxy dad for her children after their own father had died. He hadn't taken Randolph's place. No one could, but he tried, and all the children tended to go to the crusty old rancher when trouble hit.

"No one will tell me anything," she whispered. "Not even Becky. She just tells me not to worry and that they have the situation under control."

"They don't want to upset you."

"But they are," she whispered. "Not knowing is the hardest of all. Level with me, Billy Mack. Please. Give it to me straight."

"The straight of it is that you're supposed to stay calm and you're getting all riled up right now."

"I'll walk out of here tubes and all if you don't tell me what's going on, Billy Mack. I swear I will."

"Reasoning with you is like trying to put a pair of socks on a rooster."

One of the ICU nurses walked over to check on them. Lenora managed a smile as the nurse offered her a drink of water. She sipped from the straw and the nurse moved on. Lenora waited until her footsteps had faded into the far corner of the large multi-bed room.

"Did Zach really talk to Jaime?"

"He did and he said she sounded fine."

She kept her voice so low it couldn't carry past Billy Mack's ear. "Then why don't they just pay the ransom so that she can come home?"

"They're working on it."

"I don't see what there is to work on. I don't want negotiations. Give them everything they're asking for. Just get Jaime back."

"You need to let your sons handle this, Lenora. They have good heads on their shoulders and cowboy determination. You and Randolph made sure of that. They'll make the right decisions."

"I can still make the decisions for my family."

"You could, but you're not there. They are and they're grown now. You need to turn the reins over to them for this ride."

"I have a really bad feeling this time. I can't explain it, Billy, but my heart can't find any comfort no matter how hard I pray."

Desperation tightened her chest. Getting upset wasn't good for her condition, but Jaime's life was riding on this. She couldn't even imagine life without her high-spirited, exuberant daughter.

"We've been friends for a long time, Billy Mack. If that friendship means anything to you, talk to my sons and make them follow my wishes. Under no circumstances are they to take this to the FBI or any other law enforcement agency without asking me first."

"You drive a hard bargain, but I'll wag my tongue at 'em if you promise to stay in this bed and try to stay calm."

"I promise."

There was little to say after that and Lenora was actually glad when the nurse said it was time for Billy Mack to go. She closed her eyes, and her mind drifted back twenty-eight years ago to the night Zach and Jaime were born.

Randolph had sat with her in their local hospital while she was in those final clutches of labor. He'd come directly from an auction when she'd called to tell him the babies were on the way.

He'd smelled the way he so often did, of horseflesh and perspiration and that special musk that was all him. She remembered it now because it had seemed so comforting in the sterile environs of the delivery room.

When the twins had come screaming into the world, old Doctor Ed had put both of them in Randolph's arms, telling him to meet his newest children, while Lenora caught her breath from the double birth.

Randolph had stood there in all his rugged rancher strength and virility with tears in his eyes.

She'd loved him so much that night. She still did. At moments like this, she missed him as if his death had been yesterday instead of over twenty years ago.

Oh, Randolph, watch over our little girl. Take care of Jaime.

THE SUN HAD DROPPED COMPLETELY below the horizon by the time Jaime and Rio reached the lake, and the evening's first moonbeams danced across the shadowed water. She was afraid, but exhilarated. Anxious, but excited.

Rio took her arm and guided her to a cleared area that was carpeted with a thick layer of dried pine needles. Something rustled and she followed the sound to discover a family of skunks parading through the trees and toward the lake.

She stood perfectly still until they'd passed, letting the sounds and smells of the night soak in. An owl hooted overhead. Bullfrogs accompanied a chorus of tree frogs and crickets. Lightning bugs darted through the trees, and the sweet scents of earth and spring blooms perfumed the air.

Though it felt good to be out of her prison, the calm had zero effect on her pulse rate.

"What will you do if Zach doesn't know the details of the flight as yet?" she asked.

Rio propped his foot on the trunk of a downed tree. "We'll have to wait until he does."

"Perhaps you should talk to Buerto since he's handling the negotiations."

"Have you and Buerto been together long?"

"Only a few months. We met at a party for one of the charities my mother sponsors. We hit it off and before I knew it, he'd offered me a job choosing art for a five-star resort he's building in Mexico."

"Do you have experience in that line of work?"

"No. But he said I have a flair for whimsy and a style about me that was better than experience. And I am a fast learner."

"He must have made quite an impression if you just quit your current job and went to work for him."

"I was becoming increasingly dissatisfied with my job at Collingsworth Oil. Staying cooped up inside an office building for most of every day is too confining."

"Your family owns Collingsworth Oil. You surely could have had your choice of jobs there. They can't all require you to be chained to a desk."

"So said my CEO brother, Langston. But starting at the top is not the Collingsworth way. Family or not, you earn your job title. That's particularly difficult when none of the jobs curl your hair."

"So what did you do at the oil company?"

"What didn't I do would be the easier question to answer. A couple held potential, but didn't pan out."

"Which couple?" Rio asked.

He actually seemed interested, so she kept muddling through her past employment tales of woe. "I was fairly successful as a facilitator, but I couldn't get up a lot of excitement for setting up meetings. I worked the longest as a recruiter. Visiting colleges to enlist some of the brightest engineers for positions at Collingsworth Oil was fun, but I couldn't see myself doing that year in and year out. I'm not knocking it. It just wasn't me."

"So you never had a burning desire to do anything in particular?" Rio asked.

She shook her head. "I worked as a social worker for a few months after getting my degree, but I got more buried in the clients' problems than they were. My supervisor said that wasn't the key to a good client/social worker relationship. She advised me to choose another line of work. Instead I took off and spent a couple of years traveling the globe."

"I suppose you don't really have to work when you're independently wealthy."

"Not for money," she admitted. "But I want that same sense of purpose the rest of my family has. I want to do something that makes a difference in people's lives. I want to wake up in the morning excited about tackling a new challenge. I haven't found my niche yet, but I'll find it one day."

"And for now you have Buerto."

"I don't exactly have him."

"That's not how he made it sound on the phone."

"I think that's the trauma of the abduction talking. I'm fond of him, and we date. But we're not shopping for furniture." That was as blunt and as honest as she could put it.

"So back to the ransom," Rio said.

"Right." The ransom they were asking from her family. "If the cartel knew how wealthy Buerto is, I'm sure they'd be asking him to contribute to their revolting cause."

Rio reached for a branch above his head, his muscles bunching and pushing against the fabric of his shirt. "They know everything about him. He's been investigated thoroughly, the same as you, the same as your family has been. It's how the cartels work."

Which meant they'd probably been watching her comings and goings, knew when she left the office, how much time she spent with Buerto, what time she turned off her lights and went to sleep. The thought of their spying on her made her cringe.

"They knew Buerto would be with you that night," Rio explained. "Poncho ordered me to let him and Luke take care of the guy you were with. Only on the drive home did I even hear his name mentioned."

"I don't see how they could possibly know I'd be with him. It's not as if Buerto and I were together every night. And we didn't make dinner plans that night until the last minute."

"Someone had to know," Rio said, "unless…" He let the sentence trail.

"What?" she asked.

"You won't like it."

"You've kidnapped me and ruined my favorite shoes. No reason to worry about offending me with words."

He let go of the branch and took a step toward her. "Do you think it's possible that Buerto is involved with the cartel?"

"Absolutely not. He's a legitimate businessman. I'm in his office every day. If he was dealing with thugs, I'd have noticed."

"Then you've seen the receipts for the art he's purchased?"

"He hasn't actually purchased anything yet."

"So there's no proof that's why he's really in this country."

"He wants to consider all the pieces he's interested in before he actually purchases any."

"Or maybe he just created a fake profession that would let him get close to you."

"No, I'm the one who recommended he wait to do his final selection so that he'd have a more cohesive collection for the resort." Or had she? At times, Buerto did have a way of putting words in her mouth.

"I'm not accusing him of anything, Jaime. Buerto is probably as terrific as you believe he is, but I have to examine every possibility. I'll admit that as far as I know, he's not a major figure, but neither can I rule that out. Not that it would matter. If the cartel needs him, they'll use him in whatever capacity they choose."

Rio's suspicion that Buerto might be involved with the cartel sounded completely ludicrous to her. But Cutter had warned her about Rio's crazy theories. He'd also said Rio had incredible instincts for identifying trouble. "Buerto is very professional in his dealings with gallery owners," she said, feeling an obligation to defend her friend and employer. "He's nothing like Luke."

"That doesn't prove anything. The higher echelons of the cartel mix and mingle with dignitaries and some-times even presidents of countries without a miscue."

"Do you have reasons for suspecting Buerto's in-volvement other than the fact that I was with him when I was abducted?"

"A few. The way you met. The fact that he persuaded you to go to work for him when you had no experience in the business. The fact that he claims to be building a multi-million dollar resort, a profession that explains why he was only in town temporarily. And now the cartel has chosen him to act as the negotiator when there's no reason they can't go directly to your family."

"He fought to save me."

"That could have been part of the plan."

"They beat and kicked him."

"And left him alive even though he saw all of us."

"I've seen you, too." The truth of her statement hit home before the words were out of her mouth. "They don't intend for me to get out of this alive, do they?"

"Not likely." Rio stepped closer, moving into her space. "I didn't mean to upset you," he said. Not that there was any other possibility. Facing death tended to upset people. And now he was trying to tell her that her so-called boyfriend might be a thug. He backpedaled on that. "Buerto's probably just an honest guy who fell for you from the moment you met." He reached for her hand. "I can easily see how that could happen."

At his touch heat danced through her like tendrils of fire. She'd never responded to Buerto like that. She may have never responded to any man quite like that.

She struggled to think clearly, but Rio's fingers had trailed a blazing-hot path up her arm to her neck. They tangled deliciously in her hair.

"Buerto is a lucky man," he whispered almost gruffly.

But it wasn't Buerto who had her senses reeling now. Forgetting the danger, she turned her face toward Rio's and rose on her tiptoes until her lips were only a breath from his.

She wasn't sure who made the next move, but suddenly his lips were devouring hers, igniting a firestorm of need inside her. Her makeshift sarong slipped, baring her breasts. She didn't pull it up.

Rio held her close, pressing his hard, fully clothed body against her half-naked one. His hands splayed on her back. Hers wrapped around his neck. The kiss intensified until she was weak and breathless.

Then without warning Rio pulled away. He muttered a low curse and turned while she pulled the sheet back into place across her chest and tightened it.

"So much for trusting me," he said. "I had no right to push myself on you like that."

He sounded genuinely tormented. "It was only a kiss, Rio. And I initiated it." A kiss that had rocked her soul. She was still trembling from the sensual onslaught of emotions.

"I wasn't trying to get you to doubt Buerto just so that I could kiss you."

"That never entered my mind." Perhaps it should have. With all the revelations Rio had thrown at her tonight, it was difficult to distinguish reality from her own overactive imagination.

"Now that we agree that Buerto could be a problem, we should call your brother," Rio said. "You can explain to him why this second conversation with him should be kept a secret from Buerto."

"But how do I explain you?"

"With as few details as possible. Don't identify me. Just say that one of the kidnappers didn't realize what he was getting into. Assure him I'll do my level best to see to it that you get out of this alive, but that no one can know I'm trying to keep you safe."

"He'll want to know why you don't let them come and rescue me."

"Say I hate shootouts. People get killed. Tell him I'm afraid to so blatantly go against the guys I'm working for."

"And if Zach doesn't buy into this and goes to Buerto?"

"Your job is to convince him not to."

Her job. This was growing more complicated by the second. Now she wasn't just a victim; she was caught up in the duplicity.

Rio handed her the phone, but she was way ahead of him. She knew what they had to do the rest of the night. It would be incredibly risky. Regrettably, it didn't involve making love.

Chapter Seven

Zach filled his mug with coffee and walked out to the wide front porch of the big house. His brothers were inside, but he wanted to digest the information from Jaime before he shared it with them. The thought that Buerto might be involved in the kidnapping put a whole new spin on things.

It would explain why Buerto's descriptions of the abductors had been so sketchy and why he hadn't identified any of the computer-generated or photo mug shots of possible suspects Zach had made him look through. But why would a man like Buerto Arredondo become involved in such a reprehensible deed? Was he planning to steal the artwork they'd been considering and have Jaime's family smuggle it out of the country for him?

Even more perplexing was why one of the bastards who'd taken Jaime hostage would have such a sudden and drastic attack of conscience. But then Jaime did have a way of winning over everyone who met her, especially men. The guy might have fallen for Jaime.

Or he could be feeding her a giant helping of bull.

If Jaime would have just given some concrete clue as to where she was, he and his brothers could have led in a charge to rescue her. He liked action. Waiting around for someone else to call the shots was driving him mad.

Zach looked up as the rattle and rumbling of a pickup truck broke the quietness of the night. He took another sip of coffee and waited for Billy Mack to park his vehicle and meander up the walk to the house.

"Any news?" Billy Mack asked as he hit the top step.

"Some," Zach admitted. "Come inside, grab a cup of stale brew and I'll fill you in at the same time I fill in my brothers."

"Good news?"

"That remains to be seen, but it has potential, if you don't mind admitting that you might have been playing footsies with the enemy."

RIO OPENED THE BACK DOOR of the cabin and Jaime stepped inside. She felt the phone call with Zach had gone well, except that he didn't have any pertinent details about the cargo shipment. That lack of knowledge made her own plan that much more critical. Now she just had to sell Rio on it.

"If Luke's replacement isn't coming until morning, there's no reason we can't use that time to see what Buerto is really up to."

His eyebrows arched. "I'm about to put in a call to the CIA. They'll start investigating him immediately."

"It still may take days. Time is urgent, Rio. You said so yourself. We can go to his office tonight and go through all his files. I know most of his passwords. We may find the information on what they're smuggling out of the country."

"Where is this office?"

"Inside the loop. Near downtown Houston."

"In a high rise?"

He was taking her seriously. Her confidence buoyed. "No, on the fourth floor of a building just off Highway 59. There's no security guard at night. We all have pass keys that grant access to the foyer where the elevator is located and I have a key to Buerto's office unless he's changed the locks."

"There's risk involved in a break-in, Jaime. If Buerto is involved, he's associated with guys who make Luke look like Santa Claus."

"Then let's hope we don't run into them. We could run into the janitorial staff, though, so I can't show up in this sheet."

"Or in your bloody dress."

"We can stop by my house to get a change of clothes. Poncho took my purse and keys with him, but I can open my garage door with a code. I wasn't planning to be gone long so I left the door from the garage to the house unlocked."

"A lack of keys is never a problem for me, but your house could be watched."

"It's a chance we have to take, and if push comes

to shove, you have a gun. I'm guessing you know how to use it."

"You've given this a lot of thought."

"Yes. I'm not completely without guile." She started to walk away.

He caught her arm and tugged her to a stop. "If this is a woman-scorned reaction, remember that we don't know Buerto is guilty of anything at this point."

"I hope he isn't, but I need to know the truth about him. In the meantime, there are lives at stake. So what do you say, partner?"

"I'm not your partner, Jaime. I give the orders. I don't want your life in any more danger than it already is."

"Fine. What do you say, boss?"

"Let's go for it."

He yanked his dark T-shirt over his head, revealing his muscular chest sprinkled liberally with dark, curly hairs. Desire shot through her, making her light-headed.

"My shirt's clean. Wear it until we get to your townhouse. It'll fit you like a baggy dress, but will be more comfortable than that sheet that keeps baring body parts."

She looked down to see that her right nipple was exposed. Her face reddened but she left the sheet just as it was as she took the shirt from him and marched back to her bedroom to change.

The shirt smelled deliciously like Rio as she slipped into it. It was almost as if she were wrapping him around her naked body and her spirits lifted to a natural high.

She no longer felt like a prisoner, and the cabin had lost much of its oppressive qualities.

She was now an integral part of a CIA investigation and she might just have a part in bringing down members of a powerful drug cartel and stopping a deadly attack.

Even the level of danger didn't frighten her the way it should. But then Rio would be beside her every step of the way.

RIO HAD TAKEN A QUICK assessment of Jaime's River Oaks townhouse two nights ago when he'd taken part in the abduction. It was in a gated complex, landscaped with a fountain near the entry, surrounded by benches and meticulously landscaped gardens. Each townhouse had its own private drive and a three-car garage.

He'd guess her domicile to be in the million-dollar range, way out of his league. Even the hired help here probably drove newer cars than the well-used domestic sedan Poncho had left for him.

It was easy to forget she was an heiress back at the cabin but there was no ignoring it here. Yet she was sitting beside him dressed in his black T-shirt and somehow looking incredibly sexy. It fell halfway down her thighs. One shoulder was bared. Fortunately there were no nipples winking at him. He prided himself on his control in difficult situations, but he was still a hot-blooded male.

Rio scanned the area. There was no reason to expect the cartel to be guarding her house since they believed her locked inside the isolated cabin, but he was wary all the same. He pulled up in front of the townhouse and stopped in almost the exact same spot Poncho had parked two nights ago.

The house was dark. Too bad he didn't have his night vision goggles with him.

"We can pull the car inside the garage," Jaime said.

"Good idea. Give me the code to the garage door. I'll open it and you can drive in. But stay inside the car with the door locked while I make a quick inspection of the premises."

She repeated the numbers of the code. "They're my birthday. That's also the code to the alarm system."

"You need to change those to something less obvious."

"Believe me, I'll change a lot of things after this. Not that more creative numbering would have kept you from grabbing me at my door and forcing me into the backseat of Poncho's car."

He went into the garage. A sporty red BMW was parked in the far right space, leaving ample room for Jaime to pull the sedan in beside it. A motorbike that looked to be brand-new was parked on the far left. Buerto's, he assumed. He imagined the man hanging out here with Jaime, making himself at home, showering in her bathroom. Sleeping next to her in her bed.

Rio had a sudden urge to slam a fist into the man's face on general principal. If he found out he'd set Jaime up for the abduction, he'd make good on that urge and love every second of it.

He walked past the Harley as Jaime pulled into the garage. He waited until she was inside, then pushed the button to lower the door. He entered the house through the unlocked door. When the alarm began to beep, he punched in the code. Before he'd turned around completely, he heard her car door shut.

So, as expected, the little spitfire didn't follow directions, he thought.

Inside the door, he waited for Jaime. When she stepped into the townhouse, in one motion he grabbed her, pushed her against the wall, and pressed his forearm across her chest.

"That's how quickly and how easily someone could have their hands on your throat, Jaime. Next time, do as I say."

"Okay, already. I learned my lesson. Let go." She squirmed against him, trying to break free of his grasp.

With the length of his body pressed against hers, desire hit him so fast and hard that he couldn't breathe. He looked down at her blue eyes and imagined taking her right here against the wall. As tempting as the vision was, reason and safety won out.

He managed to pull away, but his body still rocked from a raw, primal desire that just wouldn't quit.

"Let's take a look at the rest of the house," he said, but his voice was gravelly and the ache in his groin was downright painful.

As they passed the laundry room, Jaime tossed her bloodied dress into the washing machine along with a pair of panties. "I simply can't put them back on unless they're clean."

"You'll have to wear the dress at the cabin," Rio said. "If Poncho sees you in something different, he'll know we left the cabin and all hell will break loose."

"I'll wear it, and when this is over, I'll bury it," she said with a shiver.

He followed her into her bedroom and this time he actually looked at the pricey furnishings. A snow-white coverlet draped the king-size bed, which was covered with an assortment of colorful pillows, all just waiting to be dived into. He tried to imagine himself living in a house this luxuriously decorated. He couldn't.

It was his cowboy roots, he told himself.

Unwanted, new images attacked his mind. The house he'd lived in with Gabrielle. The simple furnishings. She'd been so proud of the dining table and chairs he'd refinished and the crib he'd made for their coming baby.

The disturbing memory was scattered by the somber sound of Jaime's voice. "This used to be my favorite room in the house, like my own snug little hideaway. But now…I wonder if I'll ever feel safe here again."

She clutched a clean pair of jeans and a pink silky blouse to her chest. "I have to get a shower and wash my hair, but I can be dressed in a matter of minutes. There's liquor in the small bar in the study if you want to fix yourself a drink. Or if you want to grab a shower, the guest room is just down the hall."

He'd have preferred a shower with her. And here he

went again, trying to mentally fit into a saddle that would never belong to him when he had a lot more important things to deal with.

He could use that shower if he was to keep from smelling the way he had under a desert sun in perspiration-soaked fatigues. And then they'd make a call at Buerto Arredondo's office. One good clue could make all the difference.

One bit of solid information about what the cartel had planned for their Detonation Day. But all his actions had to be tempered with keeping Jaime safe. He'd promised her that, and it was a promise he planned to keep.

THE LOCK ON BUERTO'S OFFICES had not been changed. Rio followed Jaime inside, amazed at how enthusiastic she'd become about cooperating with him. She'd even brought a backpack so that they could copy any suspicious files and take the copies with them.

And two frozen gourmet pizzas in a black tote bag that she'd left in the car. The woman thought of everything.

"That's my desk," Jaime announced, pointing a flashlight beam at an uncluttered desk in the center of what appeared to be an outer office. The rest of the building was dark and they'd decided flashlights would be less conspicuous in case there was any security that Jaime wasn't aware of.

"Buerto's office is through that door on the left. There's also a large storage area and a small bathroom. Nothing is elaborate, but it's functional."

For a man interested in collecting expensive art, he had a serious lack of paintings on the light green walls, Rio noticed. The only decor in this office was a fake potted plant and a vase of white daisies. Judging from the fresh flowers he remembered seeing in Jaime's house, Rio figured she'd brought those to the office.

He picked up a folder from her inbox and skimmed through pictures of sculptures created by a Greek named Umberto Mancuso. None of which would be useful. "What were your basic duties?" he asked.

"I went with Buerto to visit the local galleries. I kept notes on the pieces of interest and then did Internet searches to see what I could find out about the artists, other works they'd done and the values of those works. If Buerto was still interested after I collected all the information, I arranged for at least two formal appraisals."

"And what did Buerto do?"

"Aside from visiting the galleries with me, I'm not really sure. He had visitors from time to time, but I got the impression they were personal friends. And he made frequent trips back to Mexico to check on his resort— if there is a resort."

"That should be easy enough for the CIA to verify. What is the name of the resort and exactly where is it located?"

"I don't remember, but I can pull it up. I do know that it looked very luxurious in the pictures. It reminded me of places I've stayed in Greece and on the French Riviera."

"Probably nothing like the barracks I've stayed in."

She looked at him with serious eyes. "But you've served your country and saved lives. I was searching for adventure. You were living one."

Leave it to an heiress to equate carrying a twenty-pound survival pack up a mountain while taking enemy fire with a vacation in exotic ports.

Jaime started typing as soon as her computer booted. "This is weird," she said. "All my files have been erased."

"They might still be lurking in the main memory. Maybe I can pull them up."

Jaime gave him her seat at the computer. He checked the usual retrieval spots. They were all empty. "Someone's deleted everything."

"I guess that proves your point. Buerto deleted the files because he never intended to buy the art, just as he never intended to see me again. The rat used me and then set me up to be killed. Now we're talking a woman scorned. He's going down."

"That's my girl. I need to get on his computer and into his files."

"Right this way." She opened the door to Buerto's office. It was considerably bigger than hers with a full executive desk and a leather swivel chair. A sea-blue plaid couch stretched along one wall. Two glass doors opened onto a narrow balcony.

"That's where he went to smoke his cigars," Jaime said. She sat down at the Buerto's computer and started typing series of numbers with no results. "Everything is password protected. I can't pull up a single file, but none of the titles seem related to art or to a resort. In fact most are numbers."

"Let me take a look at them." He set up a program to create and check thousands of password combinations, using numbers and letters.

Jaime hung over his shoulder. "You're a hacker!"

"Being a SEAL is not just about fighting and looking cool in sunglasses."

The numbers kept spinning. Finally, one of the files opened. "Bingo."

Jaime moved in closer. "That's just words put together in nonsensical patterns. It makes no sense."

"It's in code. Get me some discs so I can copy the files. I'll work on deciphering the codes later."

"You decipher secret codes!" She gave him a look of amazement. "I suppose you're also fluent in ten languages?"

"Just three." He smiled.

A new file came up, also in code. He'd need time to figure all this out and there was no guarantee he had that time.

Jaime set a box of discs at his elbow. "I'll check the file cabinet for hard copies of information."

"Super idea."

A dozen computer files opened within the next hour. The last one was a series of over one hundred names, not in code. Several of them Rio recognized from his research after taking this job or from hearing their names mentioned by cartel members. One was his CIA supervisor. All of the names he recognized were of men and women working in law enforcement in Texas border towns.

It looked an awful lot like a hit list, possibly the names of men listed for annihilation on Detonation Day.

Zachary Collingsworth was number twenty-five on the list.

Jaime was not going to take this well, he knew. He'd tell her later, once they'd finished their search in Buerto's office and were on their way back to the cabin.

By 4:00 a.m., Rio was bleary-eyed and in desperate need of a cup of coffee. He copied the last of the files and pushed away from Buerto's desk. "I think I have everything," he said.

"Good, because I didn't get much except investigative journals on me and several other women who might have been considered as victims—all of whom I know. In fact, some are good friends. All of them are from families who are rich enough to pay a multi-million dollar ransom and also have access to company planes that could have been used to ship goods. I guess I drew the lucky straw."

"There seem to be a lot of lucky straws up for grabs."

"You've been right about everything so far, Rio. I was thoroughly investigated right down to my passion for shoes and my favorite coffee shops. There's also proof that Buerto knew I'd be at the charity party that night and he knew I had a history of never staying in one job too long."

Rio stuffed the discs into Jaime's backpack. "They

play all the angles and make few mistakes. Did you make copies of the investigative reports?"

"No, but I'll get on that now." She turned to go, then stopped and looked at him. "We make a pretty good team, don't we?"

He nodded. They made a damn good team.

If he could decode these files in time, he might not even need Zach's help in discovering what would be shipped from where.

"It's a two-hour drive back to the cabin, Jaime. We should get on our way. It wouldn't do for Luke's replacement to show up and find us gone."

"You really are afraid of Poncho, aren't you?"

"No, I'm afraid of having to kill him and then get kicked from the cartel before I stop the attack."

"Two more files to copy," she said, "and then I'm ready to go."

"Okay. I'm going to the bathroom and then I'll meet you in your office."

He was passing by her desk in the outer office when he heard voices in the hall. Two men with slight accents. He recognized one as Buerto's. A key rattled in the door.

Son of a bitch. Why would Buerto be coming down to his office before daylight? It must mean the action was heating up. He had to get out of here, but the door the men were about to walk through was the only exit.

He touched his hand to the butt of gun and rushed back to get Jaime. They'd have to hide in the storage closet and hope for the best.

He slipped into Buerto's office but there was no sign of Jaime. She must have heard the voices, too. He hurried toward the closet then noticed that one of the glass doors leading to the balcony was open a crack.

Surely she wouldn't have jumped. They were on the fourth floor, with only a cement parking lot to break their fall. He lost all concern for being discovered and rushed onto the balcony. As he looked down, he saw a dark object atop a parked car.

Jaime's backpack.

Chapter Eight

Terror gripped him as his eyes wildly scanned the pavement below. There was no sign of her.

In his peripheral vision he spotted a fluttering of pink, and his heart caved in. A few feet away, just out of his reach, Jaime stood on a narrow ledge only slightly wider than her small foot, hugging the building for dear life.

He spat out a curse. Jaime Collingsworth might be afraid of roaches, but she was not afraid of anything else. Adrenaline shot through him in dizzying waves. What had she been thinking to choose such a dangerous escape method?

At least she'd had sense enough to drop the heavy backpack before she'd started walking on the treacherous ledge. And this time she was wearing rubber-sole shoes, a pair of sequined pink sneakers.

When she reached the next balcony, she caught hold of the railing and managed to swing herself onto solid footing. Only then did she look back in his direction. He gave her a thumbs-up, though what he really wanted to give her was a lecture forbidding her ever to put herself in that kind of danger again.

It hit him then that the files they'd spent collecting were lying four floors below them, the CDs no doubt smashed to pieces.

Behind him, a light went on in Buerto's office. He scooted over until he was out of sight—unless one of the men walked onto the balcony. He had no desire to take on two men before breakfast, especially now that Jaime was safely waiting for him. He threw a leg over the railing and followed her lead.

He didn't look down, but inched along. Heights didn't bother him. Falling would. When he reached the balcony where Jaime was waiting, he caught hold and climbed aboard.

She threw herself in his arms and he held her close. As he did, something poked him in the ribs. He touched the front of her blouse. "The CDs?"

She pulled them out and handed them to him. "You didn't think I was foolish enough to toss them over, did you?"

His relief was palpable. "Thank God. I'd have hated to go through all that again." He caught hold of her forearms and held her so that he could look directly into her eyes. "What the devil were you thinking when you decided to take up tightrope walking?"

"I heard Buerto's and Rafa's voices. I wasn't going to just stand there and let Buerto discover that we'd cracked his passwords and stolen his files."

"Who's Rafa?"

"I only know his first name. Buerto introduced him to me as a friend, but I think he's more likely a business associate. He comes by the office frequently. I think they'd been drinking tonight. Their voices were louder than usual."

"Even that doesn't justify your strolling along a narrow ledge four stories off the ground."

"Garth and I used to go rock climbing in Wyoming when he was participating in rodeos out there. Compared to that, balancing on the ledge was a walk in the park."

"A park in a war zone. Who's Garth?"

"An old boyfriend. Don't worry. He's ancient history." She shrugged and looked around. "Since we don't have a key to this office, can you work your magic and open the door? We need to get downstairs and recover the backpack before someone makes off with the copies."

He made quick work of the lock and they walked through an insurance office and then took the elevator to the ground floor. The buckle on the backpack had left a few nasty scratches on the top of a blue Camry. The driver would have a rough time figuring out how they got there. The backpack, however, was none the worse for wear.

Too bad Rio couldn't say the same for himself. Seeing Jaime on that ledge had stolen the elation he'd found at recovering files that could help him stop the cartels' planned attack. Her calm when he'd been so frightened for her had been downright annoying.

He couldn't figure her out. She had everything

money could buy, but instead of being a spoiled princess, she was one of the spunkiest women he'd ever met. Nothing daunted her—except roaches.

He opened the car door for her, then circled to the driver's side. Once he'd thrown the backpack into the rear seat, he got behind the wheel. He fit the key into the ignition but didn't start the motor. Instead, he stared at Jaime.

She had to be as beat as he was, but she looked as gorgeous as ever. The night had been one big adventure for her, but all he could think about when he looked at her was how easily she could have fallen to her death.

And they called him a loose cannon.

But enough was enough. His mind was made up. He couldn't keep putting her in danger, and there was only one way to guarantee she stayed safe.

"How about some food and coffee?" he asked.

"I'd love some. There's a great café nearby that serves breakfast twenty-four hours a day."

"That should work." A nice café for their last breakfast together. He'd miss her but it was the way it had to be. And there was no reason to worry about Poncho now. When Rio showed up at the cabin without Jaime, no excuse would be good enough to keep his career with the cartel from coming to an abrupt end.

Who'd have thought he could get this close to a woman in only two days? Before meeting Jaime, he wouldn't have bet ten cents that he could feel this close to a woman again in all his life.

JAIME DIDN'T REALIZE HOW ravenous she was until the waitress set a plate of eggs, bacon, hash browns and one large golden-brown biscuit in front of her. It had been a long night, and she was still stunned by all she'd learned about Buerto and Rio.

The man she'd trusted and admired had turned out to be a liar with ties to one of the most infamous Mexican drug cartels. Yet, the man who'd abducted her at gunpoint had turned out to be a former Navy SEAL currently working in a covert operation with the CIA and Homeland Security.

Buerto had set her up to be murdered. Rio had sworn to keep her alive. Her safe, pampered life had spun out of control and she'd been hurled into a world of espionage and terrorism.

She should be in a state of shock and maybe she was. That would explain the exhilaration that burned inside her. She didn't need any explanation for her attraction to Rio. He was determined, brave, smart and incredibly virile. If anyone could stop the planned attack along the border, it was he.

As for Buerto, she was furious to learn how he'd used her. Oddly, she felt no real pain at the loss of their relationship. The man she'd thought she was working for and dating had never existed. Buerto was a good-on-paper kind of guy, but everything on the paper had been lies.

"I took you for the kind of woman who'd have ordered a bowl of fruit and yogurt," Rio said when he finally took a break from his meal of pancakes, sausage and a side of Texas fries.

"Whatever gave you that idea?"

"You barely touched your food at the cabin yesterday and you're not much bigger than a newborn calf."

"I don't always eat like this, but I usually have a good appetite, especially when I'm back at the family ranch. Juanita, our cook, may be the best in the country, especially when it comes to down-home cooking with a Hispanic flair.

"My mom likes to mix gourmet fare with traditional Texas dishes. Her family Sunday brunches are to die for. As soon as this is over, I'll have you out. They'll all be eager to meet you."

Was it only a few nights ago she was finding excuses not to have Buerto meet her family? He'd managed to do that anyway, though, on his traitorous terms.

"You don't look much like a cowgirl," Rio said.

Jaime put down her fork and wiped her mouth with the napkin. "Wait until you see me in boots."

"Dressing like a cowgirl won't cut it. You know the saying. Don't call her a cowgirl until you see her ride."

"I'm an expert horsewoman, and I can do the Texas two-step in any smoky western bar. Now, tell me about you."

"I grew up on a small ranch outside El Paso. No cook. My dad, brothers and I did the wrangling. Mom took care of the house. I had a tendency to get into trouble. Nothing major, just driving too fast and partying too hardy. And playing pranks on my younger brothers."

"Do you miss the ranch life?"

"Sometimes. I figure I'll go back to it one day, when I get tired of living on the edge. That's what makes working for Cutter Martin so great. He runs the investigative and protective service from his ranch. Right now he has more work than he can handle with three SEALs already working for him."

The waitress came by, refilled their coffee cups and left them a check.

"You'll have to pay," Jaime said. "I haven't seen my purse since I threw it at you and Luke the other night."

"I'd pay even if you had your purse. I invited you to breakfast." He pulled out his wallet and took a twenty from it. "I didn't get a chance to tell you back at Buerto's office, but I found one file that wasn't written in code."

He sounded reluctant, which piqued her interest all the more. "Did it relate to the attack?"

"It's a list of over a hundred names. I only recognized a few of them, but the ones I know are all of law enforcement officers working in Texas border towns. One is my supervisor for the CIA, whose involvement in stopping the violence hasn't been publicized. Still, they have his name."

"Do you think the names are a hit list?"

"I think it's very likely. I'm not sure if those names are the extent of whatever is planned for Detonation Day, but it's a start. I'll give the information to the CIA.

They'll notify those officers so that they can be on high alert and their families can be protected."

"At least it's a start."

"We have you to thank for that."

"You discovered the file."

"Yes, but it was your idea to visit Buerto's office tonight."

She nodded her head. "I accept the kudos."

"There's more," he said. His voice had grown somber. "Your brother Zach's name is on that list."

She stared at Rio, praying she'd heard him wrong. His eyes told her she hadn't. "It's that task force he's working on. No wonder he doesn't like to talk about it. He knows it's dangerous."

"And a lot of what he's doing is likely confidential," he reminded her.

Things were suddenly a lot clearer. "That's why I drew the straw," she said. "They go after the officer and his family, so they chose me as the kidnap victim. They get the ransom and a chance to strike out at Zach's family. We have to call Zach and let him know. I won't tell him you're with the CIA or that I was in Buerto's office. I'll just say I overheard the info from the other kidnappers."

Rio handed her the phone. "I have a better idea. Tell Zach you escaped. I'll drive you to a spot near the lake where he can pick you up."

"I can't do that. If I'm not with you, then the ransom off. There will be no way we can find out what's led out of the country."

"We'll just have to go with what we have. I can't keep putting you at risk."

"But you said yourself they could be smuggling some kind of chemical for use in dirty bombs. A hundred people on a hit list is horrendous, but what if we're looking at thousands of innocent citizens including women and children?"

"It's not your job, Jaime. It's mine and all the other agents who are working day and night on this."

Rio didn't get it. She didn't fully understand it herself, but she knew what she had to do.

"All my life everything I wanted has been handed to me, Rio. It wasn't Mom's fault. She tried to instill all sorts of basic values in me, but in the end I never failed to get what I wanted. It's always been all about me. Now it isn't. I like this new me. I want to do this."

"You'll have to find something else to champion. I can't risk getting you killed by these monsters."

She raised her chin and set an expression of steely determination on her face. "It's not your risk we're talking about. It's mine. You kidnapped me and dragged me into this nightmare, Rio. Now I'm here, and I'm going back to the cabin with you and see it through."

Without any second's hesitation, she punched in Zach's cell phone number. She'd warn him his name was on that dreaded list, but that was as far as she'd go. Buerto and the others who were part of this deadly plot had to be stopped.

Finally she understood why Zach had become a deputy and why he'd volunteered for a potentially deadly task force.

He made a difference. He saved lives.

SOMEWHERE ALONG THE WAY Rio had lost complete control of Jaime, if he'd ever had it. She was dynamite in a petite, blond package. He'd known from first bite that she was a spitfire.

He knew now she was far more. *Valiant* was the first word that came to mind, a description the military reserved for their finest. They were frequently the ones who ended up dead on the battlefield. He would not let that happen to Jaime.

They were still an hour from the cabin on Lake Livingston and the sun was already beaming its first light above the gray horizon. He'd have lots of explaining to do if they arrived after Luke's replacement, but that didn't loom as his biggest problem. Decoding the CDs did.

He checked his speed. His foot was heavy on the accelerator, as usual. Slowing to just a few miles above the limit, he turned to Jaime. "Watch for a twenty-four-hour Walmart."

"Oh, goody," she said, "a shopping trip. You can buy me a pair of shoes to replace the ones you murdered."

"I'll buy you two when this is over, providing they don't cost more than ten dollars a pair."

She laughed. "When this is over I will have to introduce you to the world of Manolo Blahnik, Gucci and Jimmy Choo."

"I live for that," he teased. "Right now we need a laptop so that I can start decoding those files."

"Can you buy one at Wal-Mart?"

"I don't know, but that's the best option I can think of for shopping before dawn."

"You're in luck. I have a better option." She reached beneath her seat for the black tote that held their frozen pizza. She pulled out a laptop. "I knew we wouldn't have Internet connections in the cabin, but I'd planned to hide this under my bed and keep a journal of our mission."

"Our *highly confidential* mission." But he reached over and patted the top of the laptop. "You are now officially promoted, *partner.*"

She gave him a salute. "Unfortunately I didn't have time to recharge the battery and it's completely down. Otherwise I could drive and you could start decoding."

"That we can work around. But neither Luke's replacement nor Poncho can know we have it."

"Naturally."

Liberation from the need to purchase a laptop at sunrise freed his mind to consider the files themselves and what they could mean to the mission. His guess was that the cargo was not yet in the cartel's hands. Had it been, Jaime's family would know when and where to have that plane waiting for them.

If he or someone in the CIA could determine from the files what was being smuggled, they could possibly stop the shipment from ever reaching the cartel's hands.

Which meant he had to get these files to the CIA as soon as he got them copied onto Jaime's computer.

A handful of miles down the road, he glanced over at Jaime. She appeared to have fallen fast asleep. He'd keep his voice low, but he needed to make a couple of calls before they reached the cabin, one to Cutter and one to his CIA supervisor, Dan Camp, to let them know the latest developments.

He slid his arm across the back of the seat and let his fingers tangle gingerly in the soft curls that tumbled over her shoulder. Temptation had never looked so good— or been so wrong for him.

He'd never fit in her world. She'd never fit in his. And he would not put himself through the torture of falling in love with a woman only to lose her. He thrived on challenges and danger. His body could take them like a machine, but heartbreak destroyed the soul. He knew that all too well.

He made his calls, and his plans for the morning took a dramatic change. Never underestimate Cutter Martin. He glanced at his watch. He had thirty minutes to reach the helipad in Livingston, Texas. He should make that with about a minute to spare, give or take a few seconds. Living on frogman time.

"WAIT, JAIME. BELIEVE ME. I can save you."

Buerto was getting closer. She heard his footsteps gaining with every burning breath. But Rio was just ahead of her, his arms open, waiting to pull her to safety.

"I'm here, Jaime. Just a few more steps."

A roar exploded in her head. Gunfire. Someone was shooting at her. She turned and saw Luke, laughing raucously and firing his pistol over and over.

Rio was just ahead. She had to go on. The clattering roar grew louder and louder until...

She jerked and opened her eyes to find herself in the car with Rio. A copter hovered overhead. She'd been dreaming, but as she looked out the window, the panic she felt was real. She turned to him. "Where are we? What's going on?"

"It's okay. Cutter's in the chopper. He's meeting us so he can copy the files to deliver to a decoding expert with the CIA."

"Why didn't you wake me?"

"You needed the sleep, and I knew the racket would rouse you when the time was right."

"It could wake the dead." She retrieved the CDs as the helicopter touched down on the small airfield. Cutter jumped out, waving with one hand and carrying an oversize black briefcase in the other. He'd changed since his high school rodeo days, grown even more muscular and developed new lines and angles to his face.

He smiled as he ran toward them and the old Cutter came through. The lingering case of nerves from the dream vanished. Any familiarity in this new world she'd entered was welcome.

Cutter set the case on the ground next to the car and

exchanged a handshake with Rio before pulling her into his arms for a warm hug.

"Great work, kid." He stood back and grinned. "Only you're not quite a kid any longer."

"Neither are you," she acknowledged. "I almost didn't recognize you, but you're looking good."

"Thanks. The SEALs made a man of me. Linney keeps me smiling. Life is good."

She noticed the gold band on his left hand. "Linney must be your wife."

"Yep. A woman in a million and expecting our first child in two weeks. A girl."

"Your Aunt Merlee must be knitting like mad."

"We have enough infant sweaters to open shop." He looked at Rio. "Now we'd best get down to business before you two get caught breaking curfew. Do you have those CDs?"

"Right here," Jaime said, handing them to him. "How did you manage to get hold of a helicopter so quickly?"

"It's the first major purchase of the Double M Investigative and Protective Service. I'm in debt up to my eyeballs, but isn't she a beauty?"

"She is today," Jaime agreed.

Cutter had placed the briefcase on the hood of the car and opened it while they were talking. In minutes his own laptop was up and running, hard at work copying the files.

"I'll take these directly to the Houston airport when I leave here. A CIA agent will pick them up from me and personally carry them to D.C. They should be in the hands of the best decoder in the country by noon. Of course," he said to Jaime, "Rio may have it all figured out by then. Did he tell you about the time he saved a whole platoon by—"

"Whoa," Rio intoned. "Let's not bore Jaime with old war stories today. There will be plenty of time for that later."

"There is one thing that can't wait," Cutter said. "Langston and I haven't seen much of each other for the past few years, but I still consider him a good friend. He's all about family. All of the Collingsworths are, and I don't feel right keeping something as important as Jaime's safety from him."

"He already knows," Jaime protested. "I talked to Zach and assured him that Rio would protect me."

Rio shook his head. "There are still risks, Jaime. I've told you that. You can climb into that helicopter right now and Cutter can fly you to Jack's Bluff ranch right after he drops off the files."

"No," she said, firmly enough to leave no room for doubt.

"But I still need to level with Langston," Cutter insisted to Rio. "I want to tell him the truth about your connection with the CIA."

"They'll never give you clearance for that."

"You're under sworn oath to them right now, Rio, but I'm only under contract."

"It will change the dynamics of the investigation,"

Rio warned. "From what you've told me about the Collingsworths, I can't imagine they aren't going to insist on swooping in now to save Jaime."

"Not necessarily, but it should be their call. I'll explain that stopping a mass murder might come down to our confiscating the cargo once it had been loaded onto the Collingsworth airplane. I trust them to make the right decision, and if they decide to go through with the exchange, we can work with them on how best to get Jaime out of this alive."

"Do you have more faith in them to protect her than you do the CIA?" Rio asked.

"I'd stack them up against a small army, and there's not one of them who'd hesitate for a second to give their life for Jaime's."

"Then do what you need to," Rio said.

As they spoke, Jaime fumed. They were talking about her as if she wasn't here or didn't have the mental capacity to make decisions for herself. She didn't bother controlling her fury. "Neither of you have the right to make my decisions for me. Neither do my brothers. Tell them I said that, Cutter. Tell them that their little sister is a big girl now and I can think for myself."

"I'll be sure Langston knows that," Cutter said. "And I'm all done here." He handed Jaime back the CDs. "Take care," he said as he shut down his computer. "When this is over we'll get together and toast our success."

With his briefcase in hand, he gave Jaime a quick

parting hug. "Better watch yourself with this one, Rio. She may be after your job."

Jaime smiled. She might just be. But first she was after his bod.

THEY WERE TEN MINUTES FROM the cabin when Rio's phone rang. He'd been on his CIA phone so often this morning that he reached for it before remembering that it was on vibrate. He took the call on the phone Poncho had supplied.

"You better have a damn good excuse for not being in this cabin, Rio. And if you like breathing, Jaime Collingsworth had better be with you."

"Poncho. Great to talk to you, too."

Instantly a SEAL lesson replayed in his head: *Fortify your front, you'll get your rear shot up.*

In this case, Rio knew, the bullets would soon be flying fast.

Chapter Nine

As much as Rio would like to tell Poncho what he could do with his orders, he knew he had to placate him on the double. If he failed, he could be jerked off guard duty in the blink of one of Poncho's bloodshot eyes. His promise to keep Jaime safe would amount to no more than hollow words.

He searched his mind for an excuse Poncho might buy. "I'll tell you why I'm out with the friggin' early birds, Poncho. I was looking for a worm this rich slut you left me with would eat. She's been on a hunger strike ever since she got here. Claims that food you provided isn't fit to eat."

He glanced at Jaime and knew from her expression that she'd figured out that Poncho was at the cabin.

"So let her starve," Poncho said.

"You said to keep her alive and healthy until her family came through with the ransom."

"She'd have eaten once she got hungry enough. I'd best not find out you're lying to me, Rio. I got no use for liars. Neither does the boss."

"Yeah, well, I'm a liar, Poncho, anytime it suits my purpose. Same as you. But I'm not crazy enough to cross the boss. I like the pay."

"Are you dead sure Jaime didn't signal someone for help while you were on your food run?"

"Not a chance. She was tied, gagged and in the trunk all the time."

Jaime made a face at him. She knew what would have to come next.

"I'll see you in ten minutes," Rio said, eager to break the connection since Jaime now had his complete attention. She'd lowered her window and now she was taking off her blouse, exposing her bare chest. He was mesmerized. He'd already seen one of her nipples exposed, but as stunning as that sight was, it came in a distant second to the perfect pair of breasts pointing toward him like bullets now.

"You're killing me," he said.

"Better me than Poncho." She tossed the blouse out the window and unzipped her jeans. He slowed as she wiggled out of them and tossed them out the window, too. Naked except for a pair of silky black bikini panties, she turned and retrieved the previously bloodied dress from the backseat.

"It's still wet," she said. "But that's good. Poncho will love the story of how it was soaked with Luke's repugnant blood and how you had to watch me strip out of it and wash it in the lake."

Rio couldn't follow her logic. He could barely think

at all. Desire ran through him like a raging river, making him practically delirious.

He ached to stop the car, lay her on a carpet of pine straw and take her like some driven animal. Instead he had to tie her, gag her and throw her in the trunk.

His hands gripped the wheel. They'd grown clammy. His need had grown rock hard, pushing for release against his jeans to the point of pure pain.

He turned on the old logging road that led to the cabin, waiting to stop until he was out of view of the blacktop road they'd just left.

"Bring on the handcuffs. Time for a little S and M," she said, pulling the dress around her as she stepped out of the car.

"I've never tried that before."

"Me, either," she admitted. "Let's see what we've been missing."

"Did anyone ever tell you that you have a bizarre sense of humor?"

"A few times." She met him at the trunk, her wrap-around dress not wrapped around.

He reached for the ties. She ducked beneath his hands and snuggled into his arms before he could finish the task. "Kiss me, Rio."

Oh, God. He was not made of steel, but he wasn't jumping her bones when she was more turned on by the danger than by him. "Jaime, you're just—"

She put a hand to his mouth to stop his protests. "Don't tell me all the reasons you shouldn't kiss me, and don't start spouting remorse like you did the other night. I've been through a kidnapping, a break-in, walked a ledge four stories up and volunteered to fight crime."

The teasing had disappeared from her voice, replaced by frustration and a vulnerability that pushed him over the edge.

"Would you please just kiss me, Rio?"

A claymore couldn't have stopped him.

She responded to his ravenous onslaught, lips on lips, heat on heat. He reveled in the salty-sweet taste of her lips and the softness of her body pressed against the hard length of his passion. He fit his arms around her waist and lifted her, amazed at how light she felt.

Their tongues tangled and the kiss intensified. It was as if electricity surged through him, driving him into a frenzy of fiery need. The thought of letting go of her was like torture.

If he didn't pull away now, he never would. And so he did.

"One day we'll finish this," he told her. "When we have more than five minutes before we meet the beast."

"I'll hold you to that." She smiled saucily. "Now for the ropes and chains."

"No chains. Just ropes and duct tape."

She climbed into the trunk on her own, and he quickly tied her wrists.

"Tighter," she said. "My wrists should look as if I've been bound for longer than five minutes."

"I was trying not to hurt you."

"I can handle it."

"Superwoman." Come to think of it, the analogy wasn't too far off base.

A few minutes later they were on their way with Jaime bound and gagged in the trunk, her computer hidden beneath the seat along with the sequined tennis shoes she couldn't bear to part with and the stolen files taped to the underside of the trunk.

PONCHO WAS STANDING in front of the ramshackle cabin when Rio pulled up. He lowered his car window and waved. "Pizza delivery."

"No smart cracks, Rio. Your high jinks don't cut it with me." Poncho waited on the porch while Rio walked around and opened the trunk.

"Did you like your ride, sweetheart?" he taunted as he yanked a strip of duct tape from her mouth.

"Untie me, you creep."

Jaime played her part a little too well, kicking at him as he loosened the knot on her ankles and connecting with his wrist. When she was free, he helped her out of the car and gave her a shove toward the cabin.

She tugged on the hem of the dress that had shrunk to a length that barely covered her private parts. Poncho stared openly and it was all Rio could do not to punch those leering eyes shut.

"So the princess likes pizza," Poncho said as she climbed the rotted steps. "Where is it?"

"Ask your flunky," she replied. "I was locked in the trunk, or didn't you notice?"

"I noticed."

"When am I getting out of here?"

"We're working out the details. If your brothers play nice it could be tonight."

Rio joined them, the two frozen pizzas in hand. He held them up for Poncho to see as he followed Jaime inside. If Poncho was telling the truth, then it must mean the cargo was in their hands and ready to leave the country.

He'd have to check with Zach the second he got some privacy. He looked around the cabin. There was no sign of Luke's replacement. Dare he hope there wouldn't be one?

He tossed the pizza boxes on the table. "How's Luke?"

"Shot up bad enough that he's no use to me for now. You'd think two of you could keep one woman the size of a large teddy bear from taking your gun away from you."

"I didn't shoot him," Jaime protested. "He got fresh with me and must have mistaken his gun for something else he meant to fire off."

Surprisingly Poncho laughed at her wisecrack, easing the tension a bit before he turned to Rio. "Things are heating up fast and the boss says you'll have to take care of the babe alone. Think you can handle that?"

"You don't see any bullet wounds in me, do you?"

"No. I see you running a catering business. Don't let that happen again. You're not to leave this cabin under any circumstances until I say it's time."

"Gotcha."

"It shouldn't be long," Poncho added. "The Collings-worths are jumping through hoops to keep us happy."

"Good. I can use my bonus money."

"Right. I forget you're in this only for the money."

"Like you're not? I'm just more honest about my motivation."

Poncho ignored the remark and walked off, checking out the cabin before he announced he was leaving. Fortunately, he only glanced inside the vehicle before climbing into his own and driving away.

For Rio, being free of spying ears and eyes seemed too good to be true—which meant that it probably wasn't, especially when it was clear that Poncho didn't fully trust him.

"Can you believe—"

He cut off whatever Jaime was about to say. "That I put up with your starvation diet bull?" he ad-libbed. "You better heat up that pizza, babe, before I decide to stuff it down your throat half frozen." He strode out of the house, letting the door slam behind him.

Jaime got the message and stuck the pizzas in the oven before she followed him outside.

"Now what?"

"I've a hunch that Poncho rigged the cabin with hidden cameras or mikes."

"Why?"

"He doesn't trust me. He probably figures I'm work-ing a plan to release you for a direct payoff."

"If they don't trust you, why would they leave you in charge?"

"Evidently the man who's calling the shots does trust me. Poncho is forced to follow his orders, but if he proves that I'm working my own agenda, it would move him up a rung in the organizational ladder. More responsibility equates to more clout and more money."

"Then his leaving you without backup could be a trap."

"It could be."

"What will you do?"

"I'll check and if I find any surveillance, I'll disable them."

"Won't he know?"

"Eventually, but it's not likely there's a direct feed. By the time he figures it out, I'm hoping this will all be resolved."

"It grows more complicated by the second."

He slipped an arm around her beautiful shoulders. "Just hang tight. It's all downhill from here."

No use to mention they were likely approaching a cliff.

LANGSTON SAT ALONE AT the large oak dining-room table of the big house, letting the memories of happier times seep into his mind as he waited for the rest of the Collingsworths to join him. He'd invited the entire family this time, including the wives and his brother-in-law and his grandfather Jeremiah.

The information Cutter Martin had passed on to him was mind-boggling. The complexities of the situation drew them into a plot that could leave untold numbers of innocent people dead. And the clock was ticking.

Bart stopped in the door, holding his Stetson in his hands, his expression grim. "I got your message and came straight from the pasture. Is there bad news?"

"Jaime's still safe and Mom is still recovering, but there's news we should discuss."

"Like what? New ransom demands? Something to do with Buerto? I can tell you right now, I don't trust him."

"Good call. Let's wait on the others before I get started."

"I'll get Juanita to make a fresh pot of coffee."

"A full pot and make it strong. We're going to need it."

His wife, Trish, was the next to wander in. She'd been staying with him at their weekend cabin on the ranch since the abduction. Jack's Bluff ranch always drew them back in times of trouble.

She stopped by his chair and gave his shoulders a reassuring squeeze before taking a chair next to the windows that looked out on a row of ancient oaks. "Juanita's offered to watch the young ones during your meeting."

They could always count on Juanita. Like Billy Mack, she was as good as gold and always there when you needed her. Officially she was the cook. Unofficially she was boss of the house anytime his mother wasn't around.

"I'm glad the boys are at school today," Trish added.

"Me, too." They'd all decided that Becky's ten-year-old twins, David and Derrick, were better off out of the loop on this.

Within minutes, the rest of the group except for Jeremiah had arrived and taken seats around the table. Bart and his wife, Gina. Zach and Kali. Becky and her husband, Nick, who'd taken a few days off from his coaching job so that he could be with Becky. And Matt and his wife, Shelly.

Shelly was one of the main reasons Langston had wanted the wives present for the discussion. She'd been a CIA agent before marrying his brother, and Langston was counting on her for some inside scoop on what they could expect in the way of protection for Jaime.

Cutter was high on Rio's qualifications, but Langston still didn't like the odds of one man against a powerful cartel.

The tapping of Jeremiah's cane against the hardwood floor announced his arrival well before he reached the doorway. His booming voice quickly followed.

"Are we ready to take the cavalry in to rescue Jaime?"

"Not yet," Langston said, "but hopefully we're getting close. Sit down and I'll fill you in on the latest."

"I thought Zach was our resident cop in command," Bart said.

"He is, but the new information came from an old friend of mine, a guy named Cutter Martin. I don't know if you remember him."

"I remember him," Jeremiah jumped in. "Hell of a bronc rider when he was a kid. Competed against you, and beat your time more than once."

"Right. That's the one. He joined the Navy after I

enrolled in the Air Force Academy. He went on to become a Navy SEAL, but he's out now and running an investigative and protective service."

Zach pushed his chair away from the table. "If you want us to hire him to rescue Jaime, my vote is no. There are four of us."

"Five," Nick said. "Count me in."

"I stand corrected. There are five of us. And before we get started with this discussion, I have some information I need to pass along to all of you. I heard from Jaime again before dawn this morning."

"And you're just now telling us?" Bart questioned. "It's half past ten."

"I realize I should have come to you right away, but I needed to verify a few things first," Zach said. "Bottom line is Jaime is fully convinced that Buerto is in league with a powerful drug cartel and that he worked with them to plan her abduction."

"How did she learn that, or is this just something else the friendly abductor told her?"

"She says she overheard the kidnappers talking about Buerto."

"That could be a setup," Becky said.

Others started murmuring doubts or agreements. Langston tapped on the table to silence the group. "Let Zach finish."

This time Zach stood. "She also heard them mention a list of names that she suspects might be a hit list. I just got off the phone with my supervisor on the task force.

He checked out the information and verified that the names Jaime gave me are of law enforcement officers who work on or near the Texas border. The first four people on the list have been murdered within the last three months."

Tension seemed to suck the air from the room.

"I'd love to get my hands on Buerto right now," Bart said.

"You can't sit on this kind of information," Shelly said. "You should go to the CIA at once. They may be our only hope for getting Jaime out of this alive."

"Not our only hope," Langston put in. "That's why I called this meeting. Here's the deal."

By the time he'd repeated all he'd learned from Cutter, the group had grown uncharacteristically quiet.

Bart was the first to comment. "So it's our call? Cutter will tell you where she is right now if we want to go in and rescue her?"

"But against Jaime's will," Shelly said. "She knows the importance of stopping that cargo shipment."

"How do we know she hasn't been brainwashed by this Rio fellow?" Bart asked. "Even if he is undercover CIA. Remaining in danger instead of demanding to be rescued doesn't sound like Jaime."

"You got that right," Nick said. "I say we go in. Damn the ransom."

"Count me in," Matt said.

Jeremiah banged his cane on the floor, demanding their attention. "Have you folks all lost your minds?

Jaime's fun-loving and high-spirited, but she's as smart as any of the rest of you. Maybe smarter. Not a one of you in this room hasn't risked his life in the past few years standing up for what you believed was right.

"Well, Jaime's as good and as brave as the rest of you. When the time is right, you can all ride in with your white hats and guns blazing and bring her home safely. Until then, you let her decide the cause she's going to fight for. And saving lives seems like a hell of a cause to me."

The room grew deathly silent. Trish finally broke the spell when she stood and spoke in a shaky voice. "I stand with Jeremiah. This should be Jaime's call."

One by one, the rest of the wives stood with her. Finally even Becky joined them.

"I vote with the women and Jeremiah," Langston said, "but if we don't have the final word on the cargo pickup time and place by tomorrow morning, I think we should be open to reconsidering our plan of action."

Everyone agreed but Zach. He quietly abstained.

ZACH WAS SITTING ON THE PORCH with Langston two hours later when Buerto pulled into the driveway unannounced. His ire heated to the boiling point at Buerto's cocky swagger as he approached them. Dealing with him civilly was becoming next to impossible.

"We're making progress," Buerto said as he came up the walkway.

Langston rose from his seat on the top step. "Does that mean they're ready to talk specifics?"

"Yes, but they want a good-faith payment first."

"And yet we're the last to know," Zach said.

"I've suggested that they deal directly with you," Buerto said. "They refuse to consider it. But I've gained some measure of rapport with their spokesman. I'm convinced they're desperate, but if we meet their demands, they'll release Jaime unharmed."

"What kind of good faith payment are they looking for?" Langston asked.

"One million dollars. I warned them you might balk at the amount, but they refused to negotiate."

"Done," Langston said. "The other million will be paid when they release Jaime and not a second before."

"Tell me about the cargo," Zach said. "What size plane will they need?"

"They told me that your small personal jet would be big enough. Two of their men will accompany your pilot."

"I'm the pilot," Langston said.

"And I'm his co-pilot," Zach said. "That's not open for negotiation, either. Now, where and when?"

"They said those details would be forthcoming once they had the money in hand."

"And I'm guessing you're going to deliver that payment to them?" Zach asked.

"I don't know how the exchange will take place. I was only told to have one million dollars in cash ready the next time they called. Look, if you don't have the money, I'll pay it. I couldn't bear for them to take this out on Jaime."

Impulsively, Zach's hands knotted into fists. Buerto

was playing this to the hilt. Zach blamed himself for that, too. He should have spotted the man as a fake from the very beginning. Instead it was Jaime who'd discovered his traitorous role in all of this, along with the hit list. As of yet, he hadn't mentioned to anyone except his supervisor that his name was on that list. The family had enough to deal with.

His twin sister, working hand in hand with the CIA. He'd be proud of her if he wasn't so damned scared.

"We have the money inside," Langston said. "I'll get it for you, but let these thugs know that we're tired of waiting around. If they don't want us to go to the cops, then they'd best make plans to release Jaime into our hands within the next twenty-four hours."

"Please," Buerto pleaded, "for Jaime's sake, don't push them too hard."

For the first time in his life, Zach wanted to pull out his gun and put a bullet through a man's heart. He wouldn't, though, except in self-defense or to save someone's life. He was a Collingsworth, a cowboy and a cop—in that order. None of those creeds allowed dishonor.

But if Jaime didn't come out of this alive, he'd see that Buerto paid, even if he had to track him to the ends of the earth. And though they disagreed on how to handle the situation now, he knew his brothers would be beside him every step of the way.

THE AFTERNOON DRAGGED ON for what seemed like forever. Rio had been sitting at the computer poring over the files and scribbling notes on the back of some old paper grocery sacks they'd found in the cabinet under the stained sink. Jaime spent her time trying not to disturb him.

"You're pacing in front of me again," Rio said.

"I'm sorry. I didn't mean to distract you. I just feel so useless."

Rio shrugged. "So do I. I'm getting nowhere with this."

"Maybe we should take a walk and clear your mind."

"I'm not sure that's a good idea."

"Are you afraid of me, Rio?"

"Yep."

"What if I promise not to throw myself in your arms?"

"I'd still be afraid."

"Of what?"

"That I'd throw myself in yours."

"Would that be so terrible?"

He rubbed his eyes and stretched. "It would be great—while it lasted."

"That's good enough for me."

He closed the computer and raked his fingers through his dark hair. "Okay, Jaime. A short walk down to the lake to clear my mind, but then I have to get back to trying to crack the codes."

"I'll get my pink tennies from the car."

He laughed. "Then all the neighborhood armadillos will want sequins."

She walked onto the porch, down the steps, then stopped short at the sound of a low growl coming from the trees just beyond the cabin. A mangy black cur, so thin its bones almost poked through its skin, snarled at her without letting go of his bloody meal.

A human meal.

Shudders shook her so violently that she'd made it back up the steps before she could force the scream from her throat.

Chapter Ten

By the time Jaime had calmed down enough for Rio to make sense of what she was saying, the black stray was slinking into the woods with his prey. Jaime had been through a rough couple of days with very little sleep, he knew. A hallucination of this type wouldn't be all that unusual.

But Jaime insisted, "It was a human bone, Rio. I'm certain of it. There were even bits of what looked like ragged denim shreds on the bloody meat. The rest of the body has to be nearby. The dog looked as if it hadn't eaten for days. It might have been so hungry that it attacked and killed someone."

Rio figured that was extremely unlikely. "You stay here on the porch and I'll take a look around."

"I'm getting my shoes and going with you."

He nodded, fully aware that arguing with her was a waste of breath. Brushing a vicious horsefly from his arm, he ambled toward the wooded area. There was a clear path of blood and paw prints.

He spotted a trio of circling buzzards about a hundred yards to their east. One by one, the birds dropped out of sight and into the thickets of pine, persimmon and cottonwood trees.

When he found the buzzards, he'd find the carcass.

Jaime ran to catch up with him, her pink shoes already sporting brown streaks of earth. "You don't have your shoulder holster on."

"Look too much like Rambo when I wear it without my shirt."

"What if you need it?"

"To face a dead man? But if it makes you feel safer, I do have a gun with me, just not where you can see it."

She patted him down and when her hand touched his crotch, the stab of desire all but sent him to his knees. It was unintentional on her part. She was still too shaken to have any thoughts of sex.

"Take it easy, Jaime. There's a small pistol inside my left boot."

"I'm probably overreacting," she admitted, "but I'm anxious about what we'll find."

"You're entitled to feel anxious."

The dog's gluttonous trail meandered. Rio took a more direct path in the direction of yet another circling vulture. The remains had become a veritable forest buffet. From where he was standing now he'd say it was very near the road.

"Someone might have hit a deer," he said.

"A dear wearing jeans?" She hurried ahead of him and disappeared in the trees.

"Watch out for snakes," he called.

She slowed but continued to stay a few feet ahead of him. About the time he figured they were getting close, they crossed the trail left by the dog again.

"Oh, no!"

The vultures scattered at Jaime's cry, and Rio rushed to catch up with her. He found her standing over a body. It was not only human. It was Luke's.

Jaime stood there with her hand over her mouth. "I'm going to be sick."

He reached for her, but she brushed him away, turned and vomited at the base of a tree.

Rio had seen more than his share of bodies, some in far worse shape than Luke's. It wasn't that it had hardened him, but war had a way of desensitizing you to the shock.

He stepped closer, looking for a cause of death.

Luke was stripped to his jeans, the worn denim ragged where the starving dog had torn away the bone just below the kneecap. No shoes, meaning Luke probably hadn't walked to the crime scene. There were no visible bullet wounds, other than the one inflicted by his own gun when he'd struggled with Jaime. No signs of strangulation or head wounds.

There was evidence that the body had been dragged to the scene, apparently from the road.

"It looks as if his chest caved in," Jaime said, rejoining Rio but still looking green. "What would cause that?"

"I don't know." Rio stooped for a closer look. "I've never seen that before. It definitely didn't come from the bullet that tore up his leg."

"Do you think Poncho dumped him here to die instead of taking him to a doctor for treatment?"

"If the body had been here since yesterday, the buzzards and other animals would have done a lot more damage than what we're seeing. More likely Poncho killed him and dumped him out here this morning. That would explain his coming out for no apparent reason. No cameras. No mikes. No replacement guard."

"I don't get it. Why would he kill Luke? They seemed like friends."

"Friendships have a short shelf life in this business. Luke had been with the cartel long enough that he probably knew too much to just let him walk away if they deemed he'd lost his usefulness."

"You mean they'd shoot him over a leg wound?"

"No, but his screwing up while guarding you might have been the weight that tilted the scale against him." Or maybe they'd needed a guinea pig for a deadly chemical, and Luke was available. He wouldn't bring that possibility up just yet.

"If they can kill their friends with so little concern, it's no surprise that they can plan a Detonation Day for their enemies," Jaime said. "We have to stop them, Rio. We can't let that shipment leave the country."

A few minutes ago she'd been screaming in terror. He'd mistakenly thought she was at the breaking point.

Now she was ready to do whatever it took to get the job done. Jaime Collingsworth had amazed him again.

He slipped an arm around her waist. "Let's go back inside."

"Shouldn't we call the cops?"

"If the cops show up and drape the area in crime-scene tape, any chance of going through with the ransom payment and stopping that shipment disappears. Besides, I'm CIA. I say we save the living and I'll try to find a shovel to bury the dead. The cops can dig him up later if they like."

And when they did, the first thing they'd notice would be that his chest had literally collapsed.

Was that same fate planned for a hundred-plus law enforcement men along the border? Was that to be the theme of Detonation Day?

THERE WAS NO SHOVEL ON the premises, but Rio managed to dig the grave using a dull, rusted ax with a splintered handle he'd found in the lean-to. He'd have been tempted to leave Luke as critter feed were it not for the likelihood that his body would need to be autopsied. A chest so flat that it appeared the heart and lungs had been sucked out of it was grossly atypical.

Rio cleaned himself up at the lake, and then walked back to the cabin. The day was warm for mid-April and the sun felt good on his back.

When he didn't immediately see Jaime inside the cabin, he grew nervous. He found her stretched out on her bed, sleeping soundly, the gun he'd left her propped against the cypress-knee lamp.

The bottom of her dress had ridden up to her waist. The top was twisted so that her right breast had worked free. An animal-like hunger pummeled his senses. He inhaled quickly and wondered how he'd ever let himself become this consumed with a woman. Had she been fully clothed, he'd still long to stretch out beside her and pull her into his arms.

It had been this way when he'd first met Gabrielle. He'd never dreamed it might be this way again. But at least with Gabrielle, there had been countless similarities to bind them together. He and Jaime were total opposites.

There was nothing wrong with being filthy rich. He'd just never fit in that world. Jaime was a luxurious town-house, fancy parties, expensive clothes, exotic trips and a flashy sports car. He was a pair of Wranglers, sturdy western boots with sheaths that concealed his weapons, a hat to ward off the sun and enough challenge and danger to keep him fired up.

Jaime was hot for him now, but when the newness wore off and the current danger and excitement were over, he'd be just another old boyfriend. Ancient history, just like poor Garth.

Nonetheless, he kicked off his boots and stretched out beside her, nice and easy so as not to wake her. She shifted without waking, snuggling close. Her right leg rested on top of his, her knee nudging his organ. Her exposed breast pushed into him, the nipple cuddling with his chest hair.

Pure heaven that hurt like hell.

He closed his eyes and eventually exhaustion took hold. Numbers and letters paraded through his sleep-induced stupor like soldiers, stumbling over dead men as flat as if they'd been rolled over by a tank.

THE WIND RATTLING A KITCHEN window woke Rio. In an instant, he identified the noise and glanced at his watch. He'd slept for almost two hours. Not so terrible since he'd missed an entire night's sleep, but it was time he should have spent trying to decode the files. He'd gone a couple of days on only a few hours of sleep lots of times.

Jaime was still cocooned around him. He allowed himself the luxury of burying his face in her silky curls. The feel and fragrance of her affected him like a drug, a very addictive drug. He forced himself to ease from the bed, pick up his boots and head back to the computer.

As he worked, he remembered his dream. Marching number soldiers, moving back and forth in rank and file order… Back and forth. Not a bad idea. He opened a new file. This one was titled 244796. He gave up on the usual formulas based on most-used letters of the alphabet and the typical patterns of consonants, vowels and double letters he'd been working with.

Up two. That would make the *Y* an *A*. Back four. That would make the *P* a *T*. He kept going until the letters formed a word. *Attack.*

His spirits soared.

"Houston, we have a word."

A half hour later, he also had an acronym. RKO. It appeared several times in the file that still didn't make complete sense. There were code names for places within the code itself and number references to other files. It was as difficult to decipher as a bill drafted by Congress.

He took his phone to the front porch and put in a call to the CIA. After being switched to a half-dozen different departments, he was finally put in touch with a civilian female chemist who was familiar with RKO.

"First let me ask if you think you may have come in contact with RKO?" she asked Rio.

"No," he replied. "I'm just trying to learn about its effects on humans."

"Had you come in contact with it, you would require immediate treatment, though so far, contact has been one hundred percent fatal, at least in rats."

"Is this fatal contamination contagious?"

"No. It requires direct contact with the skin."

"Exactly what are we talking about here?"

"RKO, or so it's known, is a chemical compound that was inadvertently discovered by two science students at a university in Washington state. They were searching for a vaccine against the common cold. Their research was dropped immediately when they realized that the compound actually destroyed the heart and lungs of lab rats resulting in almost immediate death."

"Did the rats' heart and lungs actually collapse?"

"Can you hold on a minute while I verify an answer to that question?"

"Yeah. I'll hold."

Her one minute stretched to five. "I'm sorry to keep you on hold, but I didn't want to give you any false information. The data I have states that both the heart and lungs shrank to a tenth of their original size."

Just what he thought. He questioned her further. "Are there any labs in this country still working with RKO?"

"There hadn't been until recently. The fear from most responsible research scientists was the damage RKO could do if it fell into the hands of foreign or domestic terrorists. Three labs in the country now have permission to use minute amounts in their cancer research, but there are stringent restrictions on the amounts that may be stored and even more stringent protection methods to ensure it doesn't fall into the wrong hands."

Apparently not stringent enough. "I'll need the names and locations of those labs."

"I'm sorry. You'll have to get that information from the CIA."

"The CIA sent me to you."

"But only for certain levels of information."

He raked his free hand through his short hair in frustration and his voice rose. "Forget levels. We're on high alert here. RKO may already be in the hands of terrorists. Now either give me the names and locations of those labs or connect me with someone who will. Every second counts."

The bluster got him nowhere. He hung up and called

his CIA supervisor. Five minutes later he had the information on the three labs, but none of the three labs had reported missing chemicals. That wasn't good enough.

"I'll take the Culpert-Greene Research Center in Dallas," Rio said. "It's the closest of the three labs to me and the one most likely involved."

"We'll handle the other two," his supervisor added. "We can't waste any time. I need you on this like ten minutes ago."

"I'm there."

"What about Jaime Collingworth?"

"I'll have to take her with me."

His supervisor didn't hesitate. "That doesn't fit with protocol."

Rio kept his anger in check. "Do you really want to talk protocol with RKO up for grabs?"

"Forget I asked. I'll forget you told me. Just get the job done."

It was time to wake Jaime from her nap.

"I CAN'T WEAR THIS skimpy dress out in public!"

"Why not? You look great."

"For a slut. Look, Rio, I'm as hyped as you are right now, maybe more so. My brother's name is on that hit list. Buerto issued me a death warrant when he helped plan my abduction.

"But I'm not running around the state looking like I'm trying to pick up tricks. The next time you abduct a woman for the good of the country, you should tell her to pack a bag."

"You win. Get in the car. I'll stop at the first mall we come to and buy you a pair of jeans and a T-shirt."

"Fine. But I'm picking them out."

She grabbed her shoes and a bottle of water as they ran out the door. Rio rammed the car into Reverse and turned it around as she buckled herself in.

"Tell me everything that led up to the RKO discovery," she said. "Start with breaking the code."

Her fascination with him would have increased tenfold at his newest accomplishments had it not already reached its peak. She listened spellbound until he'd filled her in on every detail.

"You're brilliant, Rio."

"That's what all the women say."

"No, I mean it. Nothing gets past you. Nothing is too complicated for you. You never even think about accepting defeat."

"I'm no longer in the service, but I still live by the SEAL creed. Failure is not an option."

"Every woman in the world must want a Navy SEAL."

"We fight them off. It's how we get our combat training."

"You always tease when I try to compliment you or get serious about your personal life, Rio. When this is over, I plan to change that."

"For now, let's just deal with one battle at a time."

Rio stopped at the first mall they passed and she

picked out a pair of jeans and a pale pink sweater. She changed into them in the store's dressing room and they were on their way again in less than fifteen minutes. It was a shopping record she'd no doubt carry to her grave. Hopefully that was many years in the future.

They talked little the rest of the way. Rio seemed lost in his thoughts, and she drifted into her own as well. So much had happened since her abduction that it was difficult to believe that was only a few nights ago. No matter how this came out, she'd never be the same carefree, self-indulgent person again.

Traffic on I-45 grew exceedingly heavy as they approached the city. It was ten past seven when they reached the lab. For some reason, she'd expected it to be in a hospital. Instead it was in a brick physician's center in a cluster of medical buildings. The parking lot was nearly empty and Rio parked only a few feet from the entrance.

He'd called ahead and stressed the urgency of their visit without telling the doctor in charge of the research center exactly what he needed. A Dr. Allison Pitre was waiting for them just inside the door, along with a burly armed security guard.

"May I see your CIA credentials?" she asked Rio as soon as the introductions were past.

"I don't carry credentials. I work undercover. I'm not asking for any privileged information, Doctor. I just need you to check your secure storage unit and ascertain that no RKO is missing."

"I can't discuss the contents of our facility with you unless you bring in the appropriate credentials or arrange for someone from the CIA with the proper credentials to come in with you."

"There's no time for that. You know the capabilities of that particular compound. You know what can happen if it were to fall into the wrong hands. Check your supply now! That's an order."

The security guard pulled his gun. Rio spun, knocking it from his hand and pulling his own weapon. "Maybe I didn't make myself clear, Dr. Pitre. I've verified that you keep RKO on site. I don't want it. I just need to know that your supply is intact. If you don't check, and we find out that lives were lost because you didn't cooperate, you'll face criminal charges that could put you away for the rest of your life."

"It's a waste of time, but I'll check." Her voice and manner made no secret of the fact that she considered Rio's request ludicrous. She turned and marched through a pair of double glass doors, locking them behind her.

Rio returned his gun to his holster. The doctor was gone so long that Jaime figured she was calling the police or at least verifying his credentials with the CIA.

When the doctor finally returned, her demeanor had drastically changed. Her eyes looked haunted. Her face was pasty white and her hands were shaking. They had their answer even before she opened her mouth. The deadly chemical was officially in the hands of madmen.

Chapter Eleven

The gravity of the situation couldn't be clearer to Jaime. She'd seen Luke's body that morning. That same fate could be planned for countless innocent victims, and the pervasive horror of it had crawled inside every cell in her body.

As yet, she hadn't had the chance to talk about it with Rio. He'd let her drive when they left the research lab, but only so that he could talk on his cell phone. He'd called his CIA supervisor, then Cutter and now he was discussing the newest developments with her brother Zach. She was starting to feel like the outsider here.

She'd heard enough of the conversations to understand that RKO recovery operations were in full swing. The CIA was checking film from the lab's security cameras and checking out everyone who'd had access to the supply cabinet for the last five years.

Rio had protested not having an active role with that, but the CIA considered it more crucial that he remain at the cabin with her. Apparently they all believed that the ransom/prisoner exchange was imminent, though no one could explain why Poncho or another guard was not at the cabin with them.

Not that she was an actual prisoner as long her only guard was Rio.

The traffic was much lighter than it had been earlier and by the time Rio broke the connection with Zach, they were nearly to their cutoff.

"What's the consensus of opinion?" she asked. "Are they going after Poncho? He must have the RKO. How else could Luke have become contaminated?"

"They're conducting an all-out search for him, and if and when he shows up at the cabin, I'll let them know immediately. They'll have a team ready to swoop down and apprehend him."

"Are they watching Buerto? He might lead them to Poncho."

"They have that covered as well. The CIA is sending a team to tail him 24/7."

She checked her own rearview mirror. "Why not just confront him and demand he take them to Poncho and turn over the canister of RKO?"

"That's what I suggested. The CIA is afraid that if we make him suspicious, he'll renege on the ransom idea altogether and find another way to transport the chemical. They want him to show up at Langston's plane, RKO in hand. Otherwise, they fear we could lose control of the situation altogether."

"That's a valid consideration. The most certain way

to ensure getting the canister out of dangerous hands will be when someone boards the jet with it."

"*If* someone boards the jet with it."

She shot him a quizzical look. "I'm not following you."

"The missing canister is no bigger than a pound of coffee. If that's the only cargo, why not just drive it to the border? In fact, Poncho could already be doing that."

"But couldn't getting it across the border still be a problem?"

"Taking it across the border would make sense if they were going to use it in dirty bombs. They'd need all the materials in a place where they could work without detection. But I can't see them using RKO in any type of explosive or even a sprayer device. You heard what Dr. Pitre said."

"To what in particular are you referring?" Jaime asked. "The doctor said plenty once she realized the RKO was missing and that she'd best start cooperating."

"The part where it's believed that as little as ten grams on the skin can cause death. With such a limited supply at their disposal, why waste it by spraying an entire area with a bomb and chancing having the chemical not even hit the target? Watering it down or using pumping devices to spread it through a building's vents would be even less effective."

She frowned. "Why didn't I think of that?"

"You're not in the investigative business."

"Maybe I should be."

She felt the look he shot her. "Don't even think about it."

But she just did, and the idea didn't strike her as being that far-fetched. She was smart. She could handle a gun as well as most cops. The hours she'd spent hanging out with her brothers at the range had ensured that.

No one called her a loose cannon, but she'd never been accused of backing away from edgy adventures, either. Skiing the Alps. Diving off cliffs. Mountain climbing. Riding her Harley. She was always up for a little excitement.

And there was no law saying an agent for the CIA or for Cutter Martin couldn't wear smokin' hot shoes.

But first she had to prove herself. She thought out loud, trying to connect the dots. "So if they don't need the plane for the RKO, they must need it for something else. Which would leave us with no clue as to the location of the canister."

"Exactly."

Rio reached across the space between them and massaged her shoulder. "You've been terrific through all of this, Jaime. If we fail, it won't be because you didn't give it your all."

"I'm not through yet. I'm with you, baby. Failure is not an option."

His Poncho cell phone rang before he had a chance to respond. He groaned. "If you can't see the enemy, they're probably right behind you."

"Maybe it's time for the ransom exchange," she

said. "Or, even better, maybe he's calling to say he's waiting for us. The CIA could apprehend him and this would all be over."

But the second Rio started talking, she knew the caller was not Poncho.

"Your lover's right here with me, Buerto, in the hands of a real man, if you know what I mean." He switched the phone to speaker. "So when are you and the Collingsworths coming through with that ransom so we can get this show on the road?"

"I only wish it were up to me. I only have a minute and I need to speak to Jaime."

Rio passed her the phone. "Your boyfriend wants to make sure I'm treating you well."

"Buerto," she said, struggling to keep the revulsion from her voice. "Why hasn't my family paid the ransom? I'm sick of this cabin. I want to see you. I want to come home."

"I want to see you, too, but I can only talk with you for a minute. The kidnappers have put me through to you but they are listening to every word we say."

"Good. They can hear that I'm tired of this filthy cabin. I want to go home. I want to see you and my family."

"We have to make that happen, Jaime. The kidnappers want me to tell you that if your brothers insist on talking to you again, you must convince them not to deviate in any way from the ransom demands. Insist they don't try to trick these men. Please, Jaime. If they want you back safely, they must comply."

His words, she noticed, sounded slurred. Had he been drinking, or was he using drugs? "I'll persuade them, Buerto," she replied. "But I know them. They won't wait forever."

"I have to hang up now, but please be sure that your brothers understand the danger you're in."

What a rotten, lying, conniving rat, she said to herself. To him she said, "We all understand, Buerto."

"I'll be thinking of you, my love, until we can be together again."

"That can't come too soon for me." This time she spoke the truth. She couldn't wait to see him begging for his own life.

She killed the connection and handed the phone back to Rio. "Even hearing his voice makes me physically ill now."

"I can understand that. Did I mention that your brothers issued an ultimatum today?"

"No. When did you learn that?"

"When I was talking to Zach a few minutes ago. They told Buerto that if you aren't released within twenty-four hours, they are going to the cops. That was just after noon today."

"As if they weren't already in bed with the CIA."

"Hopefully Buerto doesn't know that."

"The ultimatum explains his call of desperation," Jaime said, "but I don't see what the cartel is waiting on."

"That's the question of the hour." He looked out the window. "Our turn onto the blacktop is coming up and the logging road isn't far after that. Why don't you pull over and let me drive?"

"I was raised on a ranch, Rio. I can drive on a cow trail."

"I was just asking."

"Okay, the answer is no. But I think you should call Poncho. I never thought I'd say this, but maybe you can lure him to the cabin."

"You are not only beautiful but cagey. That's a very dangerous combination."

"I could have told you that."

He tried Poncho. There was no answer, which was extremely unusual considering they were in the middle of a kidnapping.

It struck her that Poncho might be lying in the woods somewhere with his chest caved into a lifeless, shrunken mass.

If that was the case, the missing RKO canister could be anywhere.

EXHAUSTION SET IN BIG-TIME and Rio was dragging by the time they walked into the cabin. Poncho wasn't there to greet them this time and there was no sign he'd been around.

"I'm starved," Jaime said, opening the refrigerator.

He blamed himself. "I have this habit of forgetting about food when I'm on a mission. You should have said you were hungry earlier. We could have stopped and bought something decent to eat."

"No problem. There's bacon and cheese. I could make us a sandwich."

He moved toward the kitchen area. "I'll fry the bacon."

"No, you just sit down on the sofa and relax."

"And the role of the little woman will be played by Jaime Collingsworth."

She smiled at him. "Yes, but it's a one-night show. Don't get used to it."

He wouldn't dare.

He perched on a chair at the table and watched her work. Her energy level surprised him, considering they'd never gotten to bed last night and her nap today had only been a few hours longer than his.

"What do you say to walking down to the lake for a moonlight picnic?" she asked. "A real picnic with no talk of Poncho or Buerto or RKO. Just you and me and the quiet of the night."

He'd say it was incredibly tempting and that he owed her that much. "I'll pull a quilt off one of the bunk beds."

"Sounds perfect," she said. "Now all we need is a good bottle of wine."

"Or a nice cold beer."

"Would you settle for water?"

"If that's your best offer."

He made a pit stop and washed up. When he returned with the quilt, Jaime was packing the sandwiches and two bottles of water into one of the grocery sacks on which he'd jotted his decoding scribbles.

"I hope that mangy dog's not around," she said.

"If he bothers you I'll smash him the way I did the roach the other night."

"My big brave SEAL," she cooed, openly flirting in spite of their traumatic evening.

"*Former* SEAL," he reminded her. "But I can still handle small animals and insects." Jaime was the real challenge.

The moon was so bright there was no need for him to pull his penlight from his pocket. When they reached the lake's edge, he searched for the perfect spot to spread the quilt, finally choosing a grassy area just up-hill from the muddy bank.

They wasted no time getting to the sandwiches and his appetite kicked in at first bite. Talk was neglected in favor of nourishment. He finished his second sandwich while she was still working on her first.

His stomach full, he stretched out on his left side, propping himself on his elbow so that he could watch the moonbeams play in Jaime's strawberry-blond locks.

She was absolutely gorgeous. Feminine, flirty, seductive—even when she wasn't trying to be. It was all he could do not to pull her into his arms and resume the kiss he'd started earlier.

That would merely make it a trillion times harder to walk away before she totally broke his heart. Or before they broke each other's trying to make an impossible love affair work.

She finished her last bite of sandwich and turned to face him. "Have you ever been in love, Rio?"

"Once in every port. It's the duty of every sailor. How about you? Were you in love with Buerto?"

"Heavens, no. I thought the relationship had potential but we were still in the getting-acquainted stage. I'm glad we never made it to the bedroom stage. I'd hate to think I'd slept with that despicable, depraved subhuman. Now it's your turn again, and no avoiding the subject this time, Rio."

She stretched out beside him and his willpower turned to warm cream.

"The honest truth," she murmured. "Have you ever been in love?"

It was a simple and straightforward question. The answer was simple, too, but so intimate that he'd kept it locked away inside him and seldom shared it with anyone. Maybe it was time.

He took a deep breath and exhaled slowly. "Yeah. I was in love once."

"Only once? Tell me about her. Was she beautiful?"

"She was stunning. Long, straight hair as black as coal. Eyes even darker. A disarming smile."

He sat up and looked away, staring into a widening circle of ripples in the water. "Her name was Gabrielle and I fell in love with her the first time we met. She was sweet and caring and way too smart for me, but we were meant for each other."

"How did you know?"

"We fit. We came from the same background. We knew the same people. We even liked the same movies and read the same books. We wanted the same things from life."

"Did you marry her?"

"Two weeks after we met."

"Then what happened?"

"She was a social worker. Most of her cases involved helping Hispanic immigrant women adjust to their new life in the States. She was walking back to her car after making a home visit late one afternoon when two rival gang members across the street from her started shooting at each other."

Jaime sat up and her eyes glistened as she looked at him. "Oh, Rio, no. You don't need to say more. I wasn't thinking. I had no right to ask."

"It's okay. It's part of who I am."

She searched his face, as if gauging the truth to his statement. "Then I'd like to hear the rest."

"There's not much. One of the bullets ricocheted off Gabrielle's car and into her heart. She died instantly. So did the baby. She was eight months pregnant with our child."

Now the tears that had been gathering in Jaime's eyes overflowed onto her cheeks. "I'm so sorry, Rio. You must miss her very much."

"It almost destroyed me at the time. It's gotten easier over the years." He reached out and wiped the tears away. "It was a very long time ago, before I joined the Navy and went into SEAL training."

"And yet you're still afraid of taking a chance with someone new."

How well she read him. "I won't marry again, Jaime. I've had that once. It's too hard when you lose it. Don't expect forever and then you won't get burned."

"And you're afraid that admitting that we're attracted to each other will end up in disaster?"

"I wouldn't be if this was just an attraction, but I'm practically obsessed with you. Sometimes I'm dizzy with wanting to make love with you. If we make love, it will become a hundred times worse. Besides, there's nowhere for the relationship to go.

"You're an heiress. You live in a gold-studded world. I'm a cowboy investigator. Not a rich rancher. Just a cowboy. It's not fear that keeps me from getting sexually involved with you. It's just common sense."

She jerked away from him. "You keep telling yourself those lies, cowboy. You can hide behind your fear and call it logic, but the truth is you're a man and I'm a woman. The rest is window dressing. And if you get burned, then deal with it. It's better than just living in the cold."

She stood and yanked the pink sweater over her head and dropped it onto the quilt. Then she unzipped her jeans, wiggled out of them and bent to pull a bar of soap and a washcloth from the bottom of the grocery bag.

"I'm taking a bath in the lake, Rio. I could use you to wash my back and who knows where that might lead. If that prospect frightens you, walk back in the cabin and see if your emotional armor is enough to satisfy you tonight."

She sashayed toward the water, her shapely hips taunting him into a frenzied, feverish state. Reason flew to the wind. His defenses deserted him.

All that was left was him and Jaime and a need that was driving him insane.

Chapter Twelve

Jaime kept walking, determined not to look back. She hadn't meant to throw down the gauntlet with Rio minutes after he'd shared the heartbreaking story of losing his wife. The frustration of the moment and the emotional trauma of the last two days had gotten the better of her.

And, okay, so she wasn't used to rejection.

But their attraction for each other was on the verge of spontaneous combustion. He admitted that he was dizzy with wanting to make love with her.

And no one had ever turned her on the way Rio did. An incidental touch from him set her on fire, and she grew breathless at just the thought of his kiss.

She stepped into the water and the cold sent a shock through her system. She kept walking, the bar of soap and the washcloth clutched in her hand. The muddy bottom curled around her toes, but the wind was still and the lake's surface was as smooth as glass.

The water was nearly breast high when she heard a

splash behind her. She didn't look back. If Rio wanted her, he'd come after her.

A few seconds later she felt a tug on her legs and she was dragged beneath the dark water in a tangle of arms and legs.

Rio, at last.

He came out of the water holding her in his strong arms as if she were a drowning kid he'd just rescued. He spun around until she was drunk on the thrill of him.

"Where's the soap?" he muttered.

She handed it to him. "Don't miss any spots."

"Not a one. That's a promise."

He lowered his mouth to hers and her heart rose to her throat. There was no warm-up. The intensity was electrifying from the onset. He ravaged her mouth, desperate kisses that felt as if he could suck her into himself.

She responded with the same, her tongue jutting between his lips, tangling and teasing. She couldn't get enough, and when he stopped for breath, she trailed hot kisses across his broad shoulders.

He set her down in the water and pulled her against him, her back to his chest. He cupped her breasts, soaping one and then the other in a circular pattern that sent delicious tingles dancing though her.

When she was weak with desire, he let the soap slip from his fingers. He turned her to face him and then lifted her again, holding her up so that her breasts were level with his mouth.

Muscles bulging, he took his time, kissing and sucking

each one until the wetness inside her sexual core escaped in a heated stream. When he lowered her back into the water, she took his hand and guided it between her legs so that he could feel the fire he'd ignited.

He lifted her again and lowered her slowly, letting her ride down the full, hard length of him before he found her lips again and kissed her until her breath burned in her lungs.

He splayed his hands across her abdomen, and then let them slide lower, to her triangle of curly hair. The slow, tantalizing teasing was so seductive that she feared she'd faint.

She moaned softly and finally he slid his hand between her legs and let a finger slide inside her. Erotic shudders ripped through her. She erupted, moaning in pleasure, and still he didn't let up.

He ducked beneath the water like the magnificent SEAL he was. She gasped when he came up beneath her, his fingers finding the most exhilarating places to play. Then gripping her buttocks to hold her steady, he let his tongue explore her core.

Expectation drove her wild.

He surfaced again, trailing kisses down her neck as he guided her hand to his rock-hard erection. She fingered the tip. He shuddered and cried out her name. Emboldened, she enveloped the length of him, stroking until it throbbed in her hands.

"I want you inside me, Rio," she whispered. "I need all of you."

"You know you drive me crazy, Jaime. Completely, breathlessly crazy."

He lifted her and let her down on him slowly. His width and length filled her, and when they rocked together, her heart thundered in her chest. She cried out in delirious release when he finally rocked her home.

"And I thought you were afraid of me," she whispered when she could finally speak.

"I am. Afraid I'll never get enough of you."

"And did you?"

He smiled, his teeth shining in the moonlight. "Ask me in five minutes, over by the quilt."

"You've got yourself a date, sailor."

RIO WAS ASLEEP BESIDE JAIME when the vibration of his small cell phone woke him. He jumped to get it, and then carried it to the kitchen so as not to wake her.

"Rio, it's Dan Camp with the CIA."

Rio checked his watch. It was twenty past five in the morning. Adrenaline pumped though his system. With luck, Dan was calling to report they'd retrieved the missing chemical.

"I hate to disturb you so early, but there's a problem."

His muscles tensed. "Having to do with the RKO?"

"Indirectly. My men haven't been able to locate Buerto Arredondo to put him under surveillance. I have a full team searching for him, but so far it's a no go. There are lights on in his apartment, but no movement."

"Is it possible he fell asleep with the lights on?"

"They have the very best in surveillance equipment and the blinds are all open. If he was there, they'd know it. His car is not in its assigned parking space or anywhere else in the complex."

"What about his office?"

"Negative. And again, no car. The few cars that are in the lot have all been traced to the cleaning crew."

Cripes. There was enough RKO floating around to wipe out a small country and the CIA couldn't even locate a guy he'd talked to on the phone just last night.

"Have you heard from Poncho yet?" Camp asked.

"Not a peep, and he's not answering his phone. When are you going to break in and search Buerto's house and office for the canister?"

"When we deem it appropriate."

Meaning they considered it none of Rio's business. That wasn't good enough.

"You're procrastinating with disaster."

"We're trying to avoid disaster," Camp countered. "We have no proof at this point that the chemical is or has ever been in Buerto's hands. But if he returns and finds any clue that his house was searched, he'll bolt and run. That destroys any chance of recovering it when he boards Langston's plane."

"He may have already bolted with the canister. Or he could be in the house or office with a heart and lungs the size of a bird's and his body cold as ice. Someone else could have hightailed it with the chemical." Rio fumed.

"We're aware of that, but Buerto or someone else from the cartel showing up with it to be smuggled out of the country is still our best hope for recovering the canister."

Rio couldn't argue the logic of that, but doing nothing was never his plan of choice. "I think you're blowing valuable time. Cutter's under contract. Put the two of us on the reconnoiter mission. I'll guarantee you Buerto will not know we've been inside that house."

"I can't chance that at this point," the CIA operative countered. "And if someone involved in this sees you, you've blown any chance of the ransom exchange taking place."

"I can move without detection. I've proven that. It's why you hired me."

There was a pause. Camp was wavering. Rio went in for the kill.

"You've surely got men in place to stop Poncho and search his car for the RKO if he comes anywhere near the cabin. If that happens and you don't find the RKO, detain him until I get back here."

"You don't have to explain my job to me, Rio."

"Then turn me lose to do mine."

Still, he wavered. "It's a risk."

"So is doing nothing."

"Do you think I don't know that? But your primary job right now is keeping Jaime with you and on board to go through with the prisoner/ransom exchange."

"And to keep her safe," Rio said. "I'm sure you meant to add that."

"That's a given."

"What happened to protocol and keeping private citizens out of harm's way?"

"A stolen canister of a deadly chemical happened to it."

Dan came through loud and clear. They'd sacrifice Jaime if it came to that. Rio planned to make sure it didn't. "Does that mean Cutter and I are a go?"

"Yes, but don't screw this up, Rio."

"It's already screwed up, Dan. I'm just trying to help with the salvage operation."

"Right," Camp agreed. "Is Jaime awake? I'd like to pick her brain. I figure she may know more than anyone else about Buerto's friends and where he hangs out."

"She's asleep. Can she call you back in about five minutes?"

"Sure. Get her some coffee first. She's been through a lot. Most women would have bailed on us by now."

Jaime was not most women. It had taken Rio only days to discover that. He figured it would take a lifetime to forget it.

But right now he had work to do. He started a pot of coffee and then called Cutter. Time to take the show on the road.

JAIME WOKE TO THE SMELL of hot coffee and the sight of Rio standing over her. He was shirtless, his thick hair disheveled and a dark stubble of whiskers liberally dotting his chin. A dose of flagrant virility. She stretched and the sweet ache in her thighs let loose a wave of luscious memories.

"Good morning, gorgeous." He bent over the bed and kissed her on the mouth with only a fraction of the intensity he'd demonstrated last night.

The lack of passion and the edge to his voice was ample indication there had been news. Anxiety rolled in her stomach as she reached for the coffee cup from his outstretched hand.

"Something's wrong," she said. "What is it?"

"What kind of good-morning greeting is that?" He sat on the bed beside her and placed his hand on her bare hip, absently massaging her skin with his thumb.

"The kind of greeting a woman utters to a man who looks as if he's been dealing with the devil. Did Poncho call?"

"No, but the CIA did."

"Please don't tell me there's bad news about the RKO."

"Not if no news is good news."

In this case it clearly wasn't, she thought. "Are they tailing Buerto?"

"That's the problem. They can't locate him. He didn't go home last night, or if he did, he left before they got their act together."

"Buerto sounded as if he were under the influence when he called me," Jaime said. "Maybe he passed out somewhere. He could be with the same guy he showed up with at his office yesterday at dawn."

"The office has been dark all night."

She nodded, taking it all in. Her assessment wasn't good. "So Buerto, Poncho and the RKO have virtually disappeared."

"For the time being. And time is fast running out. So here's the deal. You, Cutter, Zach and I are going into Houston this morning to search Buerto's house for the missing canister or at least a clue as to what might have happened to it and to Buerto."

"My brother is in on this?"

"Cutter's idea. I'll explain later."

"What if Poncho shows up at the cabin while we're gone?"

"The CIA will see that he doesn't, at least not until we have a chance to get back here."

Anticipation began to take the edge off her jagged nerves. Anything beat waiting for the next deadly surprise to drop.

"It will take us at least two hours to get from here to downtown Houston in morning traffic," she warned.

"We won't be in traffic. We're meeting Cutter at the same place he landed his chopper yesterday. When we get to town, Zach will be at the helipad waiting for us in his double cab pickup."

"So that's why he's invited."

"That and the fact that he carries a legitimate badge. You never know when you might need that. Besides, Zach's a good lawman. You don't have to talk to him long to know that."

"Zach's a good man, period. Like you, Rio." She

trailed her fingers up his muscular arm. "Now let's go fight crime."

He pulled out his miniature phone. "First Dan Camp wants you to call him. They need your help."

The CIA needed her. If the situation weren't so grave, she could really savor that.

CUTTER SET THE CHOPPER DOWN on a Houston high-rise rooftop at exactly seven thirty-eight. They climbed out and took the elevator down to the street-level parking area. It took Jaime only a few seconds to spot Zach standing next to his black truck. He was dressed in his deputy's uniform and looking conspicuously authoritative. Holding back tears, she ran to him and fell into a bear hug.

"Let me look at you," he said, when she finally pulled away. His voice cracked a little.

"Don't go sentimental on me. I'll cry."

"We both might. I don't mind admitting that I was plenty scared when Buerto showed up and announced that you'd been kidnapped by three thugs. When Langston told us about the phone call from Cutter, I was gung ho to ride to the rescue."

"Thanks for not doing that, Zach. Lives are in jeopardy and I'm doing the right thing. I'm in good hands with Rio."

"You'd be in better hands at Jack's Bluff ranch."

She'd argue that point at a later time. The others had reached them and were waiting for the family reunion to end. She stepped back and made the official introductions, though once they made visual contact, Zach and Cutter vaguely remembered each other from the old rodeo days.

As soon as the hand-shaking was over, Zach opened the back door of his truck, reached inside and came out with three packages. "I have the uniforms, but I suspect Jaime's will be a bit baggy."

He passed out the packages.

"No one told me there would be baggy uniforms involved," she quipped, trying for some levity in this grim situation. "What kind of uniform?"

"A stunning two-piece number with an eye-catching pocket topped by a fashionably monogrammed exterminator emblem. And in your case, the ever-popular baseball cap in a contrasting shade of Astros red is included as a stylish accessory."

"*Me,* kill bugs? Very funny."

Zach smiled. "Yep. I saw you faint over a harmless spider once."

"It was crawling up my arm, and it didn't look harmless."

"There are restrooms in the coffee shop on the corner," Zach said, quickly getting back to business.

Rio gave him a nod of approval. "Great job."

"Dressed to kill and a latte," Jaime said. "This is my lucky day."

"Be sure and cover your hair completely," Rio reminded her.

"And leave off the hip wiggle," Zack added. "Men saunter or swagger."

She spit onto the sidewalk as she walked away, and then turned back to Zach. "How's that for manly?"

In spite of the repartee, an underlying sense of expediency prevailed. There would be no respite until the RKO was back in safe hands.

As soon as they were all back in the truck and Jaime had given Zach directions to Buerto's apartment, the conversation turned to the complications surrounding the ransom.

"I would have never thought we'd be days into the kidnapping and still not have a plan to execute the final payment," Cutter said.

Zach pulled onto a frontage road. "The ultimatum we gave them is fast approaching."

"Maybe they really only wanted the million dollars," Jaime said. "The rest could have been just to throw us off."

"I doubt that's the whole story," Rio said. "Cartels are infamous for using kidnapping as a warning or a payback. Operating funds aren't really a problem for them."

Cutter and Rio had taken the backseat, leaving Jaime to sit beside Zach as navigator. She shifted so that she could see Rio. "Maybe someone working at the research center stole the RKO and the cartel needed quick access to liquid assets to pay for it."

"That's a possibility," Rio admitted.

"Poncho could have picked it up from the thief," she

continued, thinking out loud. "He may have killed Luke with it to be certain it worked as described."

"That might be an accurate theory," Zach said, "but it doesn't tell us where that all-important canister is right now. And if we don't find that, the loss of innocent lives could be tremendous."

By the time they reached Buerto's apartment complex, the tension in the truck was almost palpable. Jaime gave Zach the security code for the front gate. He punched it in and the gate swung open.

"Have you been here often?" Zach asked.

"Buerto cooked dinner for me about once a week, and I've come alone to drop off price quotes or information he'd requested from various galleries. He didn't go into his office every day."

Zach glanced her way. "I'm sorry it worked out this way for you, Jaime. It can't be easy to realize the man you were so fond of was using you and that he had no regard for your safety."

"It infuriates me, but not for the reason you think. I know Buerto's tried to convince you otherwise, but we weren't that serious. Feel free to share that tidbit with the rest of the family."

When the entrance drive came to a crossroad, Jaime gave directions. "Go right. Buerto's apartment is in building three, a half block down on your right. He's on the third floor, 301 to be exact. Visitor and service vehicle parking is behind the building."

Zach rounded the building and pulled into the space

on the far end. "How do we do this? I don't think exterminators usually travel in packs."

"Why don't you and Cutter go first?" Rio said. "Jaime and I will follow a couple of minutes behind you. If there's any reason Jaime shouldn't go in, cut us off. And remember, put anything you move back exactly as you find it, right down to the angle of a pillow or the position of a book on a shelf."

"You don't have to coddle me, Rio. I can handle anything we run into."

He shot her a look. "Throwing up on a carpet would make it hard to leave the place exactly as we found it."

"I'm past that now. Besides, I have the key to Buerto's apartment." She held it up.

Zach snatched it from her hand. "Thanks, Jaime. And I may as well warn you, Rio. My twin sister has always been an adrenaline junkie."

Rio smiled. "I'll keep that in mind."

Rio watched until Zach and Cutter disappeared inside the building, then he shifted restlessly and stepped out of the truck. Jaime joined him. "It looks to be a nice living arrangement," he said. "Not over-the-top but classy."

"Buerto said he chose it for the convenience to his office and the roominess. I had no idea at the time that it was all for show."

"And no doubt to impress you," Rio added. "Though I'm still not sure why he felt he had to worm his way into your confidence before kidnapping you."

"Knowing how manipulative and cunning he is, I'm

sure there's method to his madness." She looked around as they moved forward. "Now that I think about it, he kept asking to go to the ranch to meet my family. Do you think that could have something to do with his luring me into his life?"

"It could be. Meeting them would give him a better idea of whether or not they'd go along with the ransom demands. Hiring you to work in a fake job still seems a bit excessive to me."

"Maybe he just wanted my body."

Rio gave her a once-over. "There's no maybe about it. He's a man? He wanted you."

"Hold on to that thought."

They took the elevator to the third floor. Rio's hand rested on the small of Jaime's back as they walked to the end of the hallway. There was no sign of trouble so he pushed Buerto's door open, glanced around and then stepped aside for Jaime to enter. His first impression was that the apartment was far too cold for human comfort. The next was a mild unpleasant odor that permeated the large open area. He locked the door behind him.

Zach stuck his head around the corner of the kitchen door. "Looks as if our guy left in a hurry. There's a half-eaten plate of food on the table and a bottle of Negra Modelo sitting next to it that looks as if it was just opened."

"I've never known him to keep the place this cold," Jaime said as she joined Cutter and Zach in the kitchen. "And he definitely never left his kitchen in a mess."

Zach opened the cabinet under the sink, pulled out and peeked into the kitchen trash can. "One Styrofoam restaurant take-out box and three empty beer bottles. It must have started out as a cold-beer kind of night. He even switched brands along the way."

"I've only seen him drink Negra Modelo," Jaime said.

"Then he may have had company."

Rio took a look at the trash. "The odd bottle is Poncho's brand." He grew more wary by the minute of what they might find. His hopes that it would be the RKO were falling fast.

Jaime leaned over the plate of food, sniffed and made a face. "Shrimp and crawfish pasta. No wonder it stinks in here."

"We should spread out and start searching for the canister of RKO," Cutter said. "I'll start in Buerto's bedroom."

Jaime followed Cutter. "I'll start in his study. He has rows of shelves in there, and a canister that small could easily be tucked from view behind books or stacks of papers."

Rio went back to the living area and looked around for the kind of unexpected niche Buerto would have chosen to hide something he couldn't afford to have discovered.

He pulled the cushions from the sofa. He found a dime and a ball of lint. There was a large flower arrangement on the mantel. The container was brass, easily large enough to hide the canister. He pulled it down and gingerly poked his finger into the moss and spongy green foam.

No luck.

Rio's attention diverted when Zach walked into the room with an oval sticker dangling from the end of his finger. He held it at an angle that enabled Rio to read it for himself.

Culpert-Greene Research Center. Extremely Dangerous. DO NOT break seal without required protection.

"I guess we can assume that Poncho made it this far with the canister," Rio stated.

Zach nodded. "But was that before or after the seal was broken and the chemical used to kill Luke?"

"My guess is before," Rio said.

The discussion was cut short by a piercing, ear-splitting yell.

Jaime.

Rio palmed his gun and took off running. This time he was afraid he'd find something much worse than a nasty insect.

Chapter Thirteen

Jaime was standing over the body. The head had fallen onto the toe of one of her sequined tennis shoes, and his dead eyes stared at her blankly. The blade of a chef's knife protruded out of his chest.

Rio holstered his weapon and put an arm around Jaime, nudging the wobbly head from her toe with his foot. So much for leaving the apartment exactly as they'd found it.

"I opened the closet door. I didn't even see him at first. He fell on top of me."

The words tumbled out of her mouth so fast she was barely intelligible. To her credit, she wasn't throwing up as before, at least not yet.

"It's okay, baby. We're all here with you."

Rio looked up and saw Zach staring at him. He dropped his arm from around Jaime's waist as if he'd been caught sneaking cookies before dinner.

Zach moved in to take over the task of comforting Jaime. He put an arm around his sister's shoulders. "Who is this?" he asked, nodding toward the corpse.

Jaime backed away from the body. "It's Poncho. He killed Luke and now Buerto must have killed him."

"Those are all assumptions," Rio cautioned.

"I think the CIA can forget waiting for Buerto to come back here," Cutter said. "His closets and drawers have been cleaned out except for one pair of muddy boots and a mismatched pair of socks."

"Then as far as I'm concerned, this kidnapping fiasco is over," Zach said. "If Poncho is dead and Buerto is missing, the cartel has more than likely cut bait and run with the RKO. The CIA had best find some other way to recover the missing chemical. They won't be putting Jaime at risk anymore."

"Poncho was stabbed," Jaime said, as if that fact was just sinking in. "His chest is bloody but not convex."

"That doesn't mean Buerto didn't have the RKO with him when he killed Poncho," Rio said. "He may have had better sense than to handle it himself. One spilled drop and the killer becomes the victim."

"We should go ahead and search the place thoroughly while we're here," Cutter said.

Rio nodded. "But first I've got to call the CIA. They can remove the body and decide what they tell the local authorities. A leak to the press about the RKO could throw the entire state of Texas into a panic."

"I think you're all jumping to conclusions," Jaime said. "Buerto never expected anyone to find the body this soon. He left the AC blasting so the smell of decay wouldn't build so quickly and alert the building super."

"What's your point?" Zach asked.

"Buerto said the kidnappers specifically requested a small plane that could take off and set down on a minimal landing strip. We have to assume they still need that and that they will follow through."

"I assume the canister of RKO is out of the area by now," Zach said. "Finding it is up to the CIA and the rest of us in law enforcement. You need to go to Jack's Bluff and stay there until things are under control."

Rio was about to agree when Zach's cell phone rang. Zach punched the talk button and then signaled for them to be silent.

"Hello, Buerto," he said so that they would all know who he had on the line. They became silent and watched his face for reaction.

"You can't be more worried about Jaime than her family is," Zach responded after a moment. "I'm ready to turn this over to the FBI. So are my brothers." Then, a few seconds later, "Are you sure they'll follow through?" He nodded to the trio in the room and said, "Just after dark. Got it. Exactly where will the exchange take place?"

Son of a bitch. Rio could only hear Zach's end of the conversation, but it was enough to convince him that Buerto was still playing the role of concerned boyfriend and negotiator. Jaime was right. The game hadn't been cancelled. He, Cutter and her brothers would need their game plan in perfect order by dusk.

Rio's own phone rang immediately after Zach's conversation ended. He figured Buerto for the caller. It wasn't. Unless he was mistaken, the voice was the one he'd heard outside Buerto's office last night, the one Jaime had referred to as Rafa.

"Okay, Rio. I'm calling for Poncho. Here's the scoop. Listen closely. I'll only say this once. You'll get another call near nightfall. When you do, follow the instructions. If for some reason you don't get the call, kill Jaime and leave her body for the buzzards."

And if he got the call, they'd still plan to kill her. The cartel had never meant for Jaime to get out of this alive.

JAIME SLIPPED HER HAND inside Rio's as they took the elevator back down to the ground floor. Thankfully, the CIA not only took care of removing Poncho's body, they also took over the search for the deadly chemical as well.

Jaime was convinced they wouldn't find it. Despite all the arguments as to why Buerto and the canister wouldn't be on Langston's plane tonight, she was still convinced that both would be there.

And she would see this through. In fact she relished the opportunity to bring Buerto down. Even if she hadn't, the need to ensure that the RKO was removed from dangerous hands was crucial. If she backed out now and the canister wasn't recovered in time to save lives, she'd carry the burden of that to her grave.

She listened as Zach and Rio exchanged the details of their calls. Langston was to have the plane ready to take off at dusk. He'd get a call giving him further directions. If the kidnappers even suspected the Collings-worths had called in any type of law enforcement, they would never see Jaime again.

As for Jaime and Rio, the orders would come later.

But the only one of her three original kidnappers still alive was Rio and he was on her side. The threat came from Buerto and the cartel. She'd put her faith in Rio over them any day.

Zach laid a hand on Jaime's shoulder. "You can ride back to the ranch with me."

"I'm sorry, Zach, but I can't. Nothing's changed except that Poncho is dead. I'm going through with this. I have no choice."

"You have a choice."

"Not one my conscience will let me make."

Zach exhaled sharply. "I knew you were going to say that. You can't blame me for trying. But if we're going to play along with these lunatics, we need to work out the details with our brothers. Why don't we meet at Jack's Bluff for lunch?"

"Works for me," Rio said. "I want Cutter included."

"Of course. He can land the helicopter near the house. The Cessna is already on the property, fueled and ready for takeoff."

"I like meeting at the ranch," Jaime said, "but what about Mom?"

Zach's lips drew into tight lines. His eyes narrowed. "What about her?"

"I know you didn't tell her I'd been kidnapped. If you

had, you'd have let me talk to her when I asked. It's okay. I'm glad you didn't put that kind of stress on her, but how will you explain our all being out there today?"

He massaged a spot on his right temple. "We didn't tell her. She heard it from Buerto right after you were kidnapped."

"Then I don't understand why you wouldn't let me talk to her."

"I didn't want to tell you this while you were being held captive, but she suffered a mild heart attack when she heard you'd been kidnapped."

Jaime stifled a cry. She felt as if the world had just come crashing down on her all over again. "How is she?"

"Recovering in the Woodlands Regional Hospital. She's been moved into a private room."

"I want to see her. I'll only stay a few minutes, but I have to let her know that I'm okay."

"Be careful how much you say. All she knows is that you were kidnapped for a ransom. She heard that from Buerto and as far as she knows he's still on our side. You can't tell her more," Zach warned. "Dr. Gathrite says she has to avoid stress."

"I won't upset her, but I have to see her." She turned to Rio. "You and Cutter take the helicopter. I'll ride to the ranch with Zach. The hospital is practically on the way."

"If you go with Zach, I go with Zach," Rio said. His tone left no room for argument. Not that she wanted to argue the point. He was a major element in the glue that was holding her together through all of this.

As Zach looked from Rio to Jaime, his expression changed. No doubt he realized their relationship had moved beyond the protection business.

"You two take my truck," he suggested. "I'll fly back with Cutter."

"We'll be there by noon," Jaime said. "Tell Juanita I can't wait for some of her homemade tortillas."

It was a lie. She had zero appetite. Learning of her mother's heart attack had sent her optimism plunging, as if realizing that her mom could reach the breaking point jeopardized her own ability to handle stress.

Not that she'd even consider backing out of her commitment. Adrenaline junkies seldom did, especially not when reaching the goal was totally worth the risk.

But even an adrenaline junkie needed to dress for the occasion.

"Two quick stops after we drop them off at the helipad," she whispered to Rio as they walked to the truck.

He shot her a speculative glance. "Tell me the first one is not for you to change into a different color of sequined shoes."

"Of course not. I'm thinking red boots with metal studs this time."

RIO WAS CONCENTRATING MORE on the predicament and considerably less on shoes when he reached the security gate of Jaime's exclusive complex. But he didn't mind stopping here.

Every SEAL he'd known had his own way of psyching himself up and releasing tension before a mission. Rio's favorite was spending time by himself. He'd been known to wander off with a six pack and not come back for hours.

If Jaime's way of coping was accessorizing, fine with him. He was so into her now, she'd have to ask to paint his toenails red or put a bow in his hair before he'd balk.

He'd always thought that if he fell for a woman again it would be someone quiet and reserved like Gabrielle had been. But the truth was he wasn't the same man he had been back then. If Gabrielle had lived, she would have changed, as well. That was life.

That didn't mean he would start believing in happy-ever-after. He was too smart for that. But he'd given up fighting the way he felt about Jaime. It was a fight he couldn't win.

"A quick shower and some fresh clothes and I'll be ready to go in a jiff," she said. "You can grab a beer and relax if you want."

"Are you sure you don't need me to wash your back?"

"The quick stop would turn into an hour of afternoon delight if you did."

And they didn't have time for that. He doubted he could even satisfy her with tonight's activity hanging over him.

She scooted out of the truck, walked to the garage and punched in the code. The door opened slowly. The garage was empty.

"That lying, cheating, murdering, thieving, rotten, no-good…"

He was by her side by the time she ran out of adjectives.

"Buerto stole my car." She threw up her hands. "And my Harley. I'll kill him."

If a change of shoes wasn't enough to relieve her pent-up tension, that outburst of fury had surely done the trick.

He pulled his gun. "Stay behind me until I'm sure the burglars aren't still inside."

"Not 'the burglars,' Rio. Buerto. He's behind this. He knows the gate code and I'm sure he watched me and memorized the garage and alarm code."

He wouldn't put anything past Buerto, but he didn't see the cartel bothering with home burglary and car theft in the middle of far more pressing matters.

For once, Jaime let him take the lead in making sure the uninvited guest was gone, but he could practically feel her seething rage as they walked from room to room. When he gave the all clear, she exploded again.

"Buerto wouldn't have known which art to strip off my walls if I hadn't told him they were originals. And he just scooped up all my jewelry—the costume and the costlier pieces. Thank goodness I keep my grandmother's locket in a safe deposit box. The heartless cad would have taken that, too."

He let her vent without attempting to stop her. It was transferred reaction. He'd seen it in the service many times. Men stayed calm and steady under enemy fire only to go crazy when someone bumped into them later and spilled their beer.

"At least he left my clothes," Jaime said. She pulled a pair of white jeans and a lilac-and-white plaid western shirt from the closet and laid them on her bed. "In honor of lunch at the ranch."

She stripped and dropped her clothes in a pile. Hot bursts of desire attacked him without warning. He fought them until he heard the water running in the shower.

Then he stripped as well, leaving his jeans lying next to hers. He swallowed hard. Even their jeans looked cozy together. This would have to be quick, but…

He pulled back the shower curtain and joined her. "I heard that they hate dirty backs at Jack's Bluff ranch."

JAIME STEPPED INTO HER mother's hospital room and her heart plunged to her toes. She considered her mother a tower of strength, but she looked pale and frail in the gray hospital gown. Even the soft clicking of the heart monitor beside her bed sounded ominous to Jaime.

She stepped closer. "Mom."

Lenora jerked and opened her eyes. "Jaime?"

She'd made a question of her name as if she didn't believe her eyes.

"It's me." Jaime hurried over and kissed her mother on the cheek. "I came as soon as I could."

"Did they hurt you? Did they—"

"No," Jaime answered quickly before her mother had time to stress. "I wasn't hurt at all. In fact one of the kidnappers took very good care of me."

Lenora smiled. "I'm not surprised. You win everyone's heart. I told your brothers to pay whatever ransom they asked. I told them not to play tough but just to get you home."

"They must have listened to you. Here I am."

"I prayed for you constantly, but I was so afraid."

"I knew you'd be praying. That gave me courage."

Lenora squeezed her hand, but the usual strength was missing from her grasp. "I wish it hadn't happened, Jaime, but the frightening memories will dim with time. We'll help with that. Maybe you and I will take a trip to Greece together. You love Greece."

Jaime rested a hand on her mother's cheek. "I do love Greece, but I'm fine. Really, I am."

"Are you sure? You seem different."

"I am different. A person can learn a lot about themselves in three days. I learned about what is really important to me. Remember when you told me that having a man of your own to love is the greatest gift in life?"

"You said you didn't need a man."

"I might have been wrong about that."

"When it's time, you'll get your man."

Jaime wished she could be sure of that. "I have to go, Mom, but I'll be back soon. I promise."

Tears wet Lenora's eyes. "I love you, Jaime."

"I know, Mom. I love you, too."

She kissed her mother's cheek and hurried out the door.

When the time came, she couldn't wait to introduce her mother to Rio.

CUTTER HAD TOLD RIO that Jack's Bluff ranch was the second largest spread in Texas. Given that and knowing that they owned Collingsworth Oil, Rio had expected their home to be much grander than the homey, sprawling house where they'd just finished the best lunch he'd had in ages, maybe in a lifetime.

The whole family was there except for Jaime's mother and her twin nephews, David and Derrick, who were in school. Apparently they'd been through a kidnapping nightmare themselves not so long ago and their parents had decided not to tell them about Jaime until she was out of danger. With luck, that would be before bedtime tonight.

One of the women whose name he couldn't remember started clearing the table. Zach's wife jumped up to help. Rio figured learning all the names of the people around the table today would be a monumental task. And for what? Chances were good Jaime would grow tired of him before he met the challenge.

"Guess we should get down to business," Zach said. "Let's retire to the back porch."

The women all stopped talking and dead silence took hold of the room. Rio realized then that the lighthearted timbre of the meal had all been feigned for Jaime's benefit. He could see the fear and confusion in the women's faces.

Her sister, Becky, finally broke the silence. She stood and threw her wadded napkin back to the table. "Okay, if no one else will say anything, I will. You're home,

Jaime. You're safe. It's crazy for you to walk back into danger and drag our husbands in with you."

Jaime stood her ground. "It might sound crazy but hundreds, maybe thousands, of lives will be lost if that canister of RKO is not found and confiscated by the authorities. I have to do what I can to help. If you were in my shoes, you'd do the same."

"This isn't the Jaime I've known all my life, and I don't like the new you." Becky pushed her chair out of the way and stormed out of the room.

"I hope you all don't feel that way," Jaime said, "but even if you do, I have to follow my conscience."

The remaining women all murmured their support, but it was still evident that they feared for Jaime.

Rio was sure he'd never met a family quite like the Collingsworths. He could definitely see where Jaime got her grit.

"Yep, my little sister is growing up," Bart said as he led the way to the porch.

"I'll make more coffee," Juanita called as they left the kitchen.

The area where they settled was more of a screened-in room than a porch. There were comfortable rockers and sofas clustered between tables and potted plants. A basket of toddler toys sat next to one of the sofas. Open shelves filled with books, DVDs and video games hugged the inside wall. The roomy porch, like the house, shouted family.

Rio took a seat on the end of the sofa. Jaime walked

over and perched on the arm next to him. "The man with the best plan wins," she said. "Ready, set, go." She yanked one of the boy's cap pistols from her waistband and pulled the trigger.

Leave it to Jaime to start what would have been a very strained meeting with a bang.

An hour and much discussion later, they agreed on the working plan that Rio had suggested at the start. Matt and Bart would be armed and hidden from sight inside the small plane's larger-than-average baggage compartment. Langston would pilot and Zach would copilot.

Cutter and Becky's husband, Nick, would be in the helicopter, staying out of sight unless more firepower was needed. If all went well, they would be there to fly Jaime home.

Everyone would have night vision goggles. Cutter had brought some extras along with him today and Zach could pick up some from the sheriff's department.

Rio would arrive with Jaime and make sure she was never in any danger.

Once Buerto or some other cartel member boarded the plane, hopefully carrying the RKO, Zach would observe his every move and give the signal to Bart and Matt when he saw an opportune time to take the man down.

They were sure the man would be armed and wouldn't hesitate to shoot anyone except the pilot, especially if they were already in the air.

Under no circumstances was Jaime to get on the plane.

It sounded workable, but Rio knew from his years

in the military that there was no such thing as a perfect plan.

But he had a good team. The Collingsworth brothers were not only smart, they had a gutsiness about them that impressed the hell out of Rio. Nick was lucky to have married into a family like this. Any man would be.

And he had no business going there, Rio warned himself. He'd been with Jaime three days. Three days of heat in the danger zone did not equate with forever.

His personal cell phone rang. He checked the caller ID. "It's Dan Camp with the CIA. I'll need to take this now." He let hope swell that they'd located the canister as he walked out and onto the back steps to take the call in private.

"What's up, Dan?"

"I have an ID on the man you knew as Poncho. His real name is Diego Gomez. And get this. His girlfriend is a tech at the Culpert-Greene Research Center in Dallas."

"Have you questioned her yet?"

"A Dallas agent is on his way to pick her up and bring her in for questioning now."

"I'd love to be there for that."

"You have a busy night. Are you sure you don't want help with that?"

"I've got a full team."

"But can you count on them the way you could our agents?"

"I do believe I can. You know, Dan, I'd really like a chance to question Poncho's girlfriend."

"I know it comes as a surprise to you former SEALs, but our regular agents can handle questioning, Rio."

"I'm not doubting you, but I'd still like a crack at her myself, even by phone. I know Poncho. I might be able to get under her skin a bit more than your guys."

"I'll see how it works out. If we don't get what we need, we'll consider giving you a call."

"I appreciate that."

A goodbye later, Rio stepped back onto the screened porch. The guys were all hoping for better news than he could give them.

Rio and Jaime spent the next fifteen minutes at the helicopter saying goodbye. Becky was the only one in the family who failed to show for a hug. Jaime didn't say it, but Rio could tell it bothered her. She kept looking back at the house.

Just as they started to hop on the chopper, Rio heard Becky calling Jaime's name. Jaime smiled and waved before they both took off running and met halfway in a bear hug.

"They are as opposite as night and day," Becky's husband said, "but when push comes to shove, they always end up together."

And then they were off. After tonight his career as a kidnapper would be over. His stint in the cartel would be over as well.

Jaime reached over and gave him a quick hug. "You survived the family," she yelled over the racket of the chopper. "Now let's go get that canister. This could be fun."

He had created a monster.

Chapter Fourteen

Rio thanked the unidentified caller and went to look for Jaime. He found her sitting on the steps of the cabin porch eating an orange she'd brought from the ranch.

"Good news," he said.

"Does that mean Buerto called?"

"No, but the same guy who I talked to this morning called back."

"Rafa?"

"I can't swear to it, but it sounds like him."

"What's the verdict?"

"You get the pleasure of riding in the trunk again."

"Oh, goody."

"I'm to have you locked away and be ready to roll by seven-thirty. I'll receive another call then to tell me where to deliver you."

She spit out a seed. "Is that it?"

Her ability to keep her emotions under control continued to amaze him. She'd had a few shaky moments when they were leaving the ranch, but since then she'd acted as if dancing with danger was a favorite pastime.

Rio sat down beside her. "I get a bonus for doing such a good job of imprisoning you."

"You earned it. How many kidnappers wash their victim's back with such enthusiasm? Was there more?"

"The caller said the Collingsworths have met all our demands and he doesn't expect any complications tonight."

"Then he's in for a surprise or two."

Rio took Jaime's right hand and wrapped it in both of his. "I know you're working hard not to let this get you down, but you don't have to put up a front with me."

"I'm not. If this was just about me, I might be. But it's bigger than that. It's about recovering that canister."

"And getting Buerto?"

"Okay, I admit it, Rio. There's a personal element to this. He used me and he used my family. He caused my mother to have a heart attack. I would love to see him locked away for the rest of his natural life.

"But mostly I'll just be glad when the action starts. I hate this waiting around."

Zach's remark about her being an adrenaline junkie might have been more truthful than he'd realized.

"Just be careful tonight, Jaime. We'll all be there to be sure things stay under control, so I don't want to see any risk-taking on your part."

"That advice from a loose cannon?"

"Do as I say, not as I do."

"You know, you'd think even the cartel would have standards. If Buerto was running the kidnapping operation, he did a shoddy job of it. He left bodies lying around. He left files on his computer that a novice hacker like yourself could break into. It took him three days to get his act together when my brothers were ready to pay the ransom during the first twenty-four hours."

"I'm not that much of a novice," he said. But she made a damn good point now that he thought about it.

In fact, it was so good that it should have occurred to him before now. The complexity of the coded files fit the standard modus operandi. The way the kidnapping was being handled didn't.

To begin with, they should have had someone more competent than Luke helping guard Jaime. They likely had no choice about using Poncho since he had the contact to get the RKO, but there should have been cameras and mics installed in the cabin so that they would know what was going on at all times.

It made it difficult to buy that this was a drug-lord operation. Yet he knew Poncho worked with the cartel. The two of them had been teamed to smuggle drugs across the border and collect cash from a couple of dealers just two nights before the abduction.

Poncho had been given the lead in that operation. That's why Rio hadn't questioned his authority when they'd kidnapped Jaime.

"You look perplexed," Jaime said. "Something rotten in Denmark?"

"I don't know, but you may have hit on something smelly in south Texas." He explained the conundrum to her as he saw it.

"Who in the cartel normally issued you orders?"

"Some guy who called himself Carlos. I'm sure it wasn't his real name."

"Is it too risky to call him, just to feel him out, I mean? You wouldn't have to mention the kidnapping to him. Wait and see if he brings it up."

Jaime's quick grasp of the situation was astounding. "I doubt I can get through to him. He gives me an emergency number when I'm taking care of business for him, but it's a different number every time."

"If he didn't give you a new number, maybe he expects you to use the same one."

"Not likely since Poncho took the original phone and issued me a new one just before we arrived at your house for the kidnapping."

"So you don't have Carlos' number at all?"

"Sure I do. I have all the numbers he's given me listed in my personal phone that Poncho didn't know about, the untraceable one I use to talk with Cutter and the CIA."

"The investigation business is high tech. I'm surprised you guys still use guns."

"Guns are like women. We never tire of them."

He tried the most recent number first. To his surprise, Carlos answered. Rio identified himself and waited.

"Where have you been, man? I've called you a dozen times."

So Carlos hadn't been in on the kidnapping. "I got hold of some bad tequila," he lied, making up the tall tale as he went. "Had this killing pain in my head. Didn't even know where I was until a couple of hours ago."

"You must have shared your bad booze with Poncho. I can't get in touch with him, either. I figured the two of you must be on a drunk together. It's okay. An occasional night of drinking is expected. Just be sure it never coincides with a job."

"No way, man. I told you, I'm disciplined. Would have gotten kicked out of the SEALs long before I did if I hadn't known how to follow orders."

"I heard you made a few orders of your own." Carlos laughed. "When you see Poncho, tell him to call in. I have a job for you two. A big job."

"On the border?"

"Right."

"What do you need us to do?"

"I'll let you know when the time is right. In the meantime, stay off the tequila—and stay available."

"I'll be ready and I'll pass the word to Poncho if I see him."

Not that he would. Nor would Poncho be drinking any more tequila.

He explained the call to Jaime.

"Then Buerto is running his own show."

"Him and Poncho, to a point. But the CIA picked up that information on Detonation Day through their usual surveillance channels so I'm not sure how Buerto's operation fits into that."

"Don't you think you should pass that new information on to the CIA and Cutter?"

He nodded.

She stood and stepped off the porch. "I'm going to take a walk down to the lake. I have a few fond memories of water, a quilt and moonlight I'd like to relive before I leave this roach-infested paradise forever."

"Give me five minutes and I'll join you." He watched her walk away, wondering how in the world he'd ever gotten lucky enough to have her fall for him even for a day. He went in the house for a bottle of cold water.

He called Dan Camp and filled him in, finishing in plenty of time to keep his rendezvous with Jaime except that Dan had other things on his mind.

"Do you still think you can get information out of Poncho's girlfriend?"

"Does that mean your guys can't?"

"No, it only means they haven't as yet."

"My time's running out here, but I'll give it a whirl if you can connect us in the next five minutes or so."

"Hold on, and let me see what I can do."

Dan was back in under a minute. "Her name's Mary Green. She's Caucasian, thirty-two years old, never married, has two kids ages two and four, one that she claims was fathered by Poncho.

"You'll be on the speaker in the interrogation room. She thinks you're behind the glass watching her. I don't give squat about why she did or didn't do anything. I just want her to admit she stole the canister for Poncho and then tell us whom he gave it to. By the way, she doesn't know he's dead."

"Does she call him Poncho or Diego?"

"Poncho. We're hooked up here."

"Let's get started, then."

"Okay," Dan said. "Ready. Set. And the speaker is on."

Rio felt the intensity in every muscle, his body reacting to the life-or-death urgency of getting this right. He wished he were there to observe the woman's body movements, read her facial expressions and look into her eyes. Going on verbal expressions alone put him at a severe disadvantage.

He played her for a few minutes, telling her he knew Poncho, making her believe he was on her side. When she warmed up to him, he upped the ante.

"I'd hate to see you go to jail, Mary. Who'd take care of your kids?"

"They can't send me to jail. I haven't done anything."

"You know Poncho's going to squeal on you when they pinch him. I like him, but he looks after number one. That's just Poncho."

"He's looking out for me, too."

"Really? From Cancun?"

"He's not in Cancun."

"Are you sure? I heard that he was. I picture him lying on the beach buying margaritas for some hottie in a bikini."

"He wouldn't have gone to Cancun without me."

"Have you talked to him today?"

"No, but—"

"Did you try to call him?"

"He wouldn't—"

"Call him. Ask him where he is."

Silence.

"He sold that canister you stole for him, Mary, and he's rolling in dough."

"You're lying. Buerto wouldn't give him the money. He was supposed to but then he wouldn't pay off, so…"

"So what, Mary? Was Poncho going to threaten him? You can't blame Poncho. A deal is a deal."

"Buerto made us do it." Her voice broke. "He kept pushing and pushing and pushing."

"How did Buerto even know you had access to RKO?"

"We met him in a bar down in Brownsville one night. I had a few drinks and I guess I must have mentioned it."

"Did Poncho mention Detonation Day?"

"No. I don't think so. Not that night."

"But he did tell Buerto about the planned mass murders?"

"He might have mentioned it. But it wasn't his fault. Buerto was on Poncho constantly, calling him all the time, buying him drinks and even giving him a fancy watch. Then he offered Poncho and me a million dollars if I'd steal a canister of RKO."

"A million dollars is a lot of money."

"That's what I mean, all that money. How could we turn it down? Buerto kept pushing until finally Poncho said we had to do it."

"So Buerto isn't with any of the drug cartels?"

"No. He's a con man. He's worked all over Mexico and even southern California. He just talks people into doing things and giving him things. He's bad and he doesn't let up."

"There's your defense, Mary. The guy pushed until you mentally broke down. You help us get the RKO back and the CIA will know you didn't mean to do it. But you have to tell them now, before people die from the chemical. Once they do, no one can save you."

"I didn't do it."

"You did it, Mary. We all know you did it. Now it's either face an electric chair or admit that you gave it to Poncho for him to sell to Buerto Arredondo."

"No, I didn't do it."

"Okay, guys. Lock her up. She'd rather fry than raise her kids. Poncho will love her for that. He'll probably send her a thank-you card. When he gets the time."

Rio heard a door open and then clang shut in the background.

"Buerto has the RKO. He's selling it to a Mexican drug cartel." Mary started to cry. "I didn't want to do it, but Poncho was going to leave me if I didn't. Now he's left me anyway."

Rio put down the phone. The CIA would take it from here. They'd have gotten the confession out of her anyway eventually. Rio was just glad he'd gotten a piece of the action.

He glanced at his watch. It was ten before seven, still time for him to walk down to the lake. He'd reached the door when he heard the outburst.

"Get your filthy hands off me, Buerto."

Rio's heart slammed into his chest. He stepped onto the porch. Buerto was dragging Jaime toward the cabin.

Rio pulled his gun. "Let go of her or I shoot to kill."

Buerto held an open vial of liquid over Jaime's head. "Kill me and you'll watch Jaime die before your eyes."

Chapter Fifteen

Jaime was forced to ride in the backseat, handcuffed to Buerto, while Rio drove. The handcuffs were to make certain she couldn't make a run for it and escape his threatening vial.

She knew from Rio's reactions that he blamed himself for this, but it was no more his fault than it was hers. She'd been lost in thoughts of Rio and hadn't heard Buerto sneak up on her through the woods.

Buerto was winning this battle. He wouldn't win the war. They'd arrest him and recover the RKO. She just wasn't sure how they were going to do it.

In the meantime, she detested the very sight, smell and voice of Buerto.

He slipped an arm around her shoulder and let his fingers brush her nipples through her shirt. She knocked his hand away.

"Does that mean you haven't missed me, Jaime? I suppose you've been too busy making out with Rio the pig."

"I haven't missed you, Buerto. I don't miss murderers and men who plot to destroy lives."

"Yet you fell for this animal who hired on to kidnap you. Have you made love to him? You have. I can tell by the way you look at him.

"I treated you like a princess for months and you only put me off with excuses of not wanting to move too fast. It took days for you to let the pig into your bed."

"You used me, Buerto. Rio protected me. It's a difference you probably can't even comprehend."

"You insult me and now the two of you plot against me. It might have worked if Poncho hadn't warned me that Rio was falling for you."

"And you killed him for his honesty? Or did you kill him because he wanted the million dollars you owed him?"

"I killed him because he was dispensable, just like you are to me now, Jaime."

"I was always dispensable to you. You came to the party the night we met simply to set me up."

"But then I met you and I wanted you for myself. I thought I might win you over and there would be no need to kidnap you. We could have lived the good life on your money. But you were never into me."

Thank God for that. "Where's my Harley? And my BMW?"

"Well taken care of."

Rio checked them out through the rearview mirror. "When's Detonation Day, Buerto? Isn't that your baby?

Sell the idea to the cartels and then provide them with a little handy dandy canister of fun and games?"

"You flatter me, Rio. I didn't dream up Detonation Day, I just took advantage of an opportunity, the way you did this week with Jaime. But the CIA got hold of the information, so now it's all been called off."

"And you lost a sale. But that still leaves you the Collingsworth money. That'll buy a lot of tequila."

"One never totally loses a sale as long as he possesses the merchandise. Turn right at the next road," Buerto said. "Jaime and I have a plane to catch."

Jaime's confidence took a nosedive as they started down the deserted road. She'd imagined them going to a small airport where there would be people around. She hadn't thought it through. If they had a landing site on their spread for a small plane, surely other ranches did, too.

"The road dead-ends ahead. Turn left when it does," Buerto said. "We won't have long to wait. In fact Langston should be waiting on our arrival."

Rio slowed the car. "Jaime hasn't done anything to deserve this. Leave her and take me with you. I'll work for you. I'm good at what I do. I can find a buyer for the RKO."

"Sorry, Rio, but deadly chemicals are easy to sell. New offers are coming in every day. Terrorists love its qualities and some of them are suicidal enough to actually use it. I'm just waiting until the price is right."

"You have the heart of a devil," Jaime said.

"Yes, my dear, but as soon as Langston's aircraft

touches down in Mexico City, you and your brothers will have no heart at all."

Rio made the turn. There would be no waiting. The Cessna had already landed.

PANIC WAS MOUNTING FAST as Rio stopped near Langston's plane, parking so that his lights would illuminate a path to the door. Langston and Zach would have on the night goggles and with the full moon, that was all they'd need. His goggles were back at the cabin, as useless to him as their plans.

"Open the door for us," Buerto ordered.

Rio did and held it while Jaime got out. He squeezed her hand quickly. He should say something to reassure her, but his mind drew a total blank.

Buerto scooted out of the car after Jaime. "Now put my bag on my shoulder."

Rio hesitated. Buerto stared at him and tilted the open vial.

Not willing to risk a spill, Rio carefully lifted the small bag and placed the strap over Buerto's shoulder. Rio was certain it contained the missing canister, yet there was nothing he could do but let Buerto walk away with it.

"Take the bullhorn from the front seat beside you and warn Jaime's brothers that the two of us are coming on board. They are to stay in their seats. One wrong move by anyone and enough RKO will be spilled on Jaime to ensure her instant death."

Rio did as he was ordered, his mind frantically searching for a way to keep Jaime and that canister off of the airplane.

Plans are only blueprints to be filled in as needed by true leaders.

His first team leader had drilled that into Rio's head and he'd never forgotten it. He'd made lots of failed plans work under enemy fire. He had to find a way to do it one more time. He could not lose Jaime this way.

He stepped out of the car and watched as Buerto and Jaime walked toward the plane. He got a glimpse of the minimal landing strip. It appeared to be a road to nowhere, perhaps the site of a housing development that died before it got past the road-building stage. That had happened in several places when the housing market crashed.

Leave it to Buerto to find a dark, deserted spot like this. His blueprint was intact.

Jaime's head was held high and her back, arrow straight, as if she were the one in total control. Rio pointed his gun at Buerto. He could easily put enough bullets in the shoulder bag to destroy the canister but the spray of chemicals would kill both Jaime and Buerto.

There had to be another way. Once she stepped inside that plane, her safety would be out of his hands. Once the canister was on that plane, an incalculable number of people could die, starting with Jaime and her four brothers.

Cutter and Nick would fly into the rescue, but there

would be nothing they could do. One vial of RKO and a man of unspeakable evil had claimed all the power.

Jaime climbed the first narrow step with Buerto right behind her. Impulsively Rio's finger tightened on the trigger. He worked for the CIA. His job was to keep the deadly chemical from leaving the country. His conscience demanded he stop it from disappearing into enemy hands at any cost.

His heart felt only desperation. He could not lose Jaime.

Still he held the gun steady, his finger poised on the trigger and ready to shoot.

In the blink of an eye, Jaime went down hard on the plane's steps and Buerto fell on top of her. Jaime's hand came up and slammed into the vial. The liquid seemed to spray from it in slow motion. The images of the drops falling on Jaime imbedded in Rio's mind.

A cry of agony tore from his throat as he raced to the plane to hold Jaime in his arms.

Buerto was on his feet again by the time Rio got there. He yanked his gun from the holster and aimed it at Jaime. Rio exploded. He kicked the gun from his hands and then slammed Buerto's head against the side of the plane. When he looked up, four Collingsworths had their guns aimed at Buerto.

Rio grabbed Jaime and pulled her into his arms. "I'm so sorry, Jaime. So sorry." His voice cracked and his eyes burned.

"Then kiss me," she whispered, "and I'll think about forgiving you, especially since you just saved my life."

"The vial of—"

"Water. It was only water, wasn't it, Buerto? You played a bluff and you lost."

"It almost worked. If you hadn't tripped, it would have."

"I didn't trip. Now will someone find the key and unlock me from this monster? And take that bag from him, Zach, before he drops the canister of RKO and kills us all."

Rio kissed her hard, not sure his heart had started beating again yet. "How did you know?" he asked when he came up for air.

"I didn't at first. But then I thought about his saying that some terrorists were suicidal enough to actually handle RKO. Buerto has no regard for anyone else's life, but he's not suicidal. That's why he killed Poncho with a knife."

"That was a damn risky thing to try, Jaime."

"I know. I'm really glad it worked."

"I love you, Jaime Collingsworth."

"I love you right back, Rio Hernandez. Now get up and help them arrest Buerto so that you can take me home. I have a very dirty back."

JAIME SAT BACK AND RELAXED. It had been one hellacious night, but finally she knew exactly what she wanted to do for the rest of her life.

All that was left was to convince Rio to go along with it.

Chapter Sixteen

The first Sunday in May was Lenora's homecoming. The whole family, including Rio, was at Jack's Bluff ranch to celebrate. He wasn't officially family, but Jaime could live with that.

The day was gloriously sunny and delightfully mild. Since no one could compete with Lenora's Sunday brunches, they'd decided to have a barbecue. The men had smoked a large brisket, pounds of ribs and four chickens.

The women had made potato salad, baked beans and Trish's famous chocolate cake to go with the home-made ice cream they'd churn later. Jaime's job had been to warm the rolls. They were only slightly burned.

Rio fit in amazingly with her family, especially her brothers and Nick. In fact, he fit in almost too well. The men were monopolizing all of Rio's time with questions when she had other plans for him.

"So Buerto is spilling the beans all over the place," Bart said. "Interesting, considering he was so macho when things were going his way."

"Let me see if I have this straight," Nick said. "Rafa is a childhood friend of Buerto's who just happens to be in a position of authority in the cartel."

"Right, and when Buerto questioned him about selling the deadly chemical to the cartel, he thought the timing was perfect, considering that Detonation Day was in the advanced planning stage."

"And then he stole the files for Buerto," Langston said, "all for a piece of the ransom?"

"Exactly."

"Has Rafa been arrested?" Zach asked.

"He has, and I think they have enough on him and on Carlos to put them both away," Rio said. "Unfortunately, that won't make a dent in the cartels. It's going to take a lot more work to bring them down."

"But they won't have the canister of RKO at their fingertips and neither will any other terrorists," Nick said. "And they have apparently called off Detonation Day. I'd say you and Jaime did a hell of a job. There's no telling how many lives you saved."

Rio beamed. "Jaime deserves most of the credit. You should hear the CIA singing her praises." He looked around, spotted her and smiled.

Jaime smiled back. She'd already decided that this was the day that she'd approach Rio with her proposition. Now that she'd made the decision, she couldn't wait to confront him.

He wouldn't protest too loudly with all the family around and she wouldn't be too tempted to hurl one of her gorgeous new Jimmy Choo red high-heeled sandals at him if he said no.

So why was she still so nervous?

Finally Rio left her brothers and walked over to where she was standing.

"There's a new foal," she said. "Take a walk with me to the horse barn and I'll show him to you."

"You can walk though hay in those shoes?"

"I walk quite well in these shoes." She added an extra wiggle to her sway to demonstrate.

But now that she'd got started she couldn't wait until they reached the barn. She took his arm and tugged him to a stop beneath oak tree. "I've been thinking about our capturing Buerto and recovering the RKO."

"Really? I try hard not to think about that night."

"We made a great team."

He pulled her into his arms. "We *make* a great team."

"Yes, but we're not fully a team."

He tipped his Stetson. "Is this where I'm supposed to fall on my knee and pull out a ring?"

"No, it's where I'm supposed to quit beating around the bush and say what's on my mind."

His eyebrows arched. "So this the scene where you dump me?"

"Absolutely not. But you know how I said I'd never found my passion in a career?"

"I recall that."

"That's changed. I now know what I want to do with my life."

"Am I supposed to guess?"

"I want to be an investigator, and don't laugh. I know I have a lot to learn but I'm a fast learner."

"I think that's a—"

"Wait. I haven't finished. I've already talked to Cutter. He likes the idea. He thinks I have potential and great intuitive skills even under pressure."

"I'd have to agree with that."

"He says I showed great moral courage."

"I'd drink to that."

"He says I'd be an asset to the Double M Investigation and Protection Service."

"I can't argue with that."

She took a deep breath and held it. "I'd like it if we were partners on a case sometime."

"Fine by me, as long as you don't throw yourself in the path of danger."

"Then you don't think my becoming an investigator is a ridiculous idea?"

"No, but you don't need my permission to do anything you want, Jaime. You're a free spirit. I love that about you, but—"

She groaned. Why did there always have to be a but?

"While we're talking partners, I think we should go all the way." He dropped to one knee and pulled out a ring.

She stared at him in shock.

"I love you, Jaime, with all my heart. I have since the first day we met. I will until the last day of my life."

"And I love you, Rio, so much that I can't even imagine life without you in it."

"Will you marry me, Jaime?"

Her heart tripped madly and she could swear the earth moved beneath her feet. Still… "What about those things you said about never wanting to be married?"

"They were spoken by a fool. I finally wised up." He stood and pulled her into his arms. "You haven't answered my question yet."

Her heart was so full her chest could barely contain it. "Yes. That would be a definite yes." She couldn't wait to tell the world and especially her mom.

Jaime Collingsworth had finally got her man.

* * * * *

& INTRIGUE...

0211/46a

INTRIGUE...

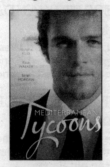

No, please don't.

Nashville homicide lieutenant Taylor Jackson is pursuing a serial killer who leaves the prior victim's severed hand at each crime scene.

TV reporter Whitney Connolly has a scoop that could break the case, but has no idea how close to this story she really is.

As the killer spirals out of control, everyone must face a horrible truth: that the purest evil is born of secrets and lies.

www.mirabooks.co.uk

2 FREE BOOKS
AND A SURPRISE GIFT

We would like to take this opportunity to thank you for reading this Mills & Boon® book by offering you the chance to take TWO more specially selected books from the Intrigue series absolutely FREE! We're also making this offer to introduce you to the benefits of the Mills & Boon® Book Club™—

- **FREE home delivery**
- **FREE gifts and competitions**
- **FREE monthly Newsletter**
- **Exclusive Mills & Boon Book Club offers**
- **Books available before they're in the shops**

Accepting these FREE books and gift places you under no obligation to buy, you may cancel at any time, even after receiving your free books. Simply complete your details below and return the entire page to the address below. You don't even need a stamp!

YES Please send me 2 free Intrigue books and a surprise gift. I understand that unless you hear from me, I will receive 5 superb new stories every month, including two 2-in-1 books priced at £5.30 each and a single book priced at £3.30, postage and packing free. I am under no obligation to purchase any books and may cancel my subscription at any time. The free books and gift will be mine to keep in any case.

Ms/Mrs/Miss/Mr _____ Initials _____

Surname _____

Address _____

_____

_____ Postcode _____

E-mail _____

Send this whole page to: Mills & Boon Book Club, Free Book Offer, FREEPOST NAT 10298, Richmond, TW9 1BR.